a separate

God

LUCINDA
STREIKER-SCHMIDT

a separate

God

Journal of an Amish Girl

TATE PUBLISHING & Enterprises

Published by Tate Publishing & Enterprises, LLC
127 E. Trade Center Terrace | Mustang, Oklahoma 73064 USA
1.888.361.9473 | www.tatepublishing.com

Tate Publishing is committed to excellence in the publishing industry. The company reflects the philosophy established by the founders, based on Psalm 68:11,
"The Lord gave the word and great was the company of those who published it."

Book design copyright © 2008 by Tate Publishing, LLC. All rights reserved.
Cover design by Kellie Southerland
Interior design by Stephanie Woloszyn

Published in the United States of America

ISBN: 978-1-60604-676-0
1. Fiction
2. Religious
08.05.09

dedication

For Tim and Lisa, my children, whom I love more than life.

acknowledgements

First and foremost to my astonishingly brilliant, gifted children, Tim and Lisa, who have always believed in me and are my best friends.

To my dear friend and ally, Josie Cohen, my eternal gratitude for her monumental help during the editorial process.

To my sister and friend Laura, who has offered her unending support and encouragement.

To the outstanding team at Tate Publishing for their faith and superior guidance.

To Janey Hayes, author acquisitions editor at Tate who believed in me from the start.

To the many dear friends who bless my life and who

have always been there with support, tolerance, and encouragement.

Last, but not least, to my parents John and Susan Schmidt and the Amish culture who were the inspiration for this book.

foreword

Many years have passed since I completed *A Separate God* and yet more years since I left the Amish Society. When I was a child I frequently asked my mother if people on the outside had a separate God because they could do things we could not do. She always told me, "You think too much." After a time I stopped asking.

I wrote the text from a journal I kept since childhood and then shelved it, too fearful and ashamed to allow anyone to read it. To this day I find it painful to read. It is an excruciating reminder of leaving the only world I knew and a seemingly unending struggle to adapt to the world I live in now. I can scarcely remember what it was like to be an Amish girl, even though I will always be one.

I have learned that true strength and courage come from God. Additionally, I now know that I do not have to be, and never will be the perfect girl/woman. And that is okay.

I recognize that I was conditioned from infancy by an authoritarian society that espoused the marginalization and trivialization of women. For years, I have struggled with damaged self-worth, crippling mood disorders and a suffocating need for male approval resulting in severely impaired decision-making, poor judgment, and emotionally scarring choices.

With a concentrated effort I have labored at overcoming doubt, guilt, shame, and self-loathing, turning it instead into the positive energy of self-affection and respect, acceptance and tolerance (God loves me the way I am, why shouldn't I?). With great difficulty and courage I acknowledged this monumental truth and my self-perception began to change. I recognized that I could be instrumental in helping the women of my people come to this realization as well. Their contribution to their children, family, and friends——indeed, the world they live in is profound and should never be overlooked or taken for granted.

As my recognition of self-worth increased so did my desire to comfort, teach, and empower the women of my culture and indeed, all women.

It is imperative to note that the disturbed, socially sick behavior that I was a victim of, perpetuated by some of the people in my life, is by no means the norm of the Amish; it tends to be more prevalent in a closed society because of the protection such a culture provides. These women and children have no support systems, help lines, or resources to turn to. *They have no voice.* All is swept tidily under the carpet and not spoken of again.

It came to light, years later, that Margaret's child (who is now grown and whom I feel complete and utter compassion for) may have been her father's child, who was reputedly, also molesting her. To my knowledge, neither she, nor her family ever speak of it or have ever addressed the situation. Ignoring it is apparently far less disturbing.

I will always carry with me the beauty of my childhood and the love of my reverent mother and father. They love their children, despite the sometimes flawed manner with which they displayed their devotion. I know that although some of their decisions were misguided, perpetuated by the generations before them, they were always filled with good will, integrity, and honor. I love them more than words can express. I love my people, and will always be grateful for not only the values instilled in me, but for the pain that shaped me into who I am today. I have a far greater understanding of the human condition and humility that comes not from joy and ease but from life—trials and difficulties.

Every day is a gift, each moment is precious, and I will seize it with both hands and clutch it tightly to my heart.

introduction

Near Berne, Indiana, where the author was born and raised, is a place called Amishville. The owner, a former Amish member, converted his farm into a park, now a major tourist attraction. And they come; the tourists do, from coast to coast, mesmerized by the quiet, earthy charisma of "The Plain People." They marvel at the simplicity of the Amish habit, the horse-drawn carriages, and the efficiency of the households, run as they are, without electricity or telephones.

Jacob Ammon, an elder in the Swiss Brethren Mennonite Church of Europe, founded the Amish Church in the seventeenth century. The first American Amish community was founded in 1817, in Butler County, Ohio. Since then, many communities, too numerous to count, have emerged throughout the United States, Canada, and South America. Each of these communities yield to Amish doctrine as their basic teaching, but with minor variations. For example, some communities may allow indoor plumbing, covered carriages, and interior decoration, while others will adhere more strictly to the principles.

Because of the European heritage, the common language spoken is German, or more accurately, a dialect of German known as Pennsylvania Dutch.

The Amish, as a homogeneous community, stubbornly cling to standards that separate them from the Great Society. The Amish life is primarily guided and controlled by the "regel und ordnung" (rules and regulations).

These rules, too lengthy and numerous to explain, are all encompassing in their power to regulate and direct the manner in which the Amish dress, worship, keep their homes and educate their children. The foundation for their structured, disciplined lifestyle is taken from their reverent view of themselves as a "peculiar people" (Titus 2:14, NIV).

Their concept of all that is "worldly" or deviant from "the way of the forefathers" is that it is devil-inspired. Their aversion to vanity clearly speaks for itself in the manner in which they dress and in the stark simplicity of their homes. Most Amish members consider it not so important to comprehend the rules they follow as to blindly obey them.

Baptism into the church takes place at approximately sixteen years of age, at which time the youth not so much makes a personal commitment, but is channeled into the act by family and social pressure. There are exceptions, of course, and some youth choose to join the church at their own bidding. Preceding baptism, the youth attends instruction classes where the church elders strenuously and forcefully teach the eighteen articles of faith, stressing the importance of obedience to the church "regel und ordnung." Minor infractions or deviations committed by a baptized member are amended by the erring one making a public confession at Sunday services. However, when a member deviates to the point of a lifestyle change, hence forsaking Amish doctrine, excommunication is imminent and unavoidable. At that time, the shunning practice of "meidung" begins, which prevents the excommunicated member from eating and drinking with, as well as, giving gifts to Amish members.

As a former member of the Amish church, the author's life was at one time centered on the views of "regel und ordnung" that many of her people still cherish and obey. *It is highly important to note here that the author's views of the Amish faith are her own, and as such, infinitely subjective. In no way are the views herein meant to judge, defame or slander the Amish society. The author's story is meant only to describe the conflicts and experiences that one person confronted as a member of the Amish faith. A Separate God is a work of fiction, based on a compilation of true events.*

Although all incidents and characters are based upon fact, some parts were revised to facilitate better emphasis and clarification.

Book One

prologue

Even though it is still early on Saturday morning, the rough, cobbled streets of Shipshewana are already buzzing. The local Amish farmers come to town early, anxious to finish their business before the heat of midday.

Already the air is heavy, somnolent with grain and dust from the earth hitching area where the farmers tether their horses and park the black, covered buggies. The sound of creaking leather, rattling carriage wheels, and automobile engines mingle, compete, and then merge in this town, little more than a village. Shipshewana, Indiana, only one of the many central locations of the various Amish communities, happens also to be a major tourist attraction.

They come from miles around, the "outside" people, the "wretched tourists," and marvel at the simplicity of the Amish lifestyle. They wonder at the horses and carriages while picking their way delicately around the horse droppings on the streets as they pursue yet another look or even a photograph of the quaintly dressed Amish folk.

A little boy, three or four, trips over the curb and skins his elbow. He sobs quietly and fitfully rubs his fists over his eyes. His mother exits the 1930's style yard-goods store carrying a package. She likely purchased some white organdy for a new cape and apron or a prayer covering. Or perhaps, she purchased some linen for a new dress; dark it would be and made from a stark, simple pattern—modest to the point of vanity.

The mother approaches the injured, weeping child and calmly, gently pulls him to his feet, soothing his elbow with ministering fingers. She also has with her another child, maybe two years old, and together, the three walk slowly back to their carriage in the hitching area. She pauses momentarily to adjust the suspenders that keep slipping off the little boy's shoulders and then refastens a button that came undone on his homemade, denim trousers. The two-year-old, a tiny, fine-boned baby girl is dressed almost identically to her mother. They are wearing the traditional female Amish habit: calf-length dress of solid color, plain black shoes and stockings, and white organdy prayer covering.

The mother, obviously pregnant, draws closer to where I sit, the pine bench beneath the shade by the hitching area.

I marvel, nearly envying the peace and contentment on her ageless face. She looks almost ignorant, but not quite naive, sheltered nonetheless.

That could be me. Memories flash in front of my eyes; they shudder and waver. For one fleeting moment I am back on the farm in Berne, that magnificent Amish homestead, and I am wearing the clothes this Amish woman wears, doing the work of an Amish maiden.

So long ago—centuries ago.

My two children bring me abruptly out of my musings as they saunter towards me from the ice cream parlor across the street. Phillip, a fourteen year-old Adonis, brandishing symmetrical features, bronzed to an enviable copper by the California sun, is intent on savoring every bit of the homemade ice cream they have purchased.

Regina moves with the studied, sylph-like grace of a dancer (extensive investments in tap and ballet by her parents). At twelve, she already shows signs of hypnotic beauty and wears her Guess and Gitano with a blithe, natural flair.

Products of private prep schools they are—only the best—Mike insisted on it. And preppies they are. Phillip's lissome, well-formed frame is clothed in OP and Adidas, complete with $120.00 Nike Airs.

They sit beside me and stare in mesmerized silence at the ever-present, ever-preserving Amish women, men, and children, going here and there in the creaking carriages.

"I used to live that way," I explained. They gaze at me—their mother, who looks no different from any mom of the other kids at school or in the vineyard country of Northern California, had once looked like them?

We make our way slowly to our car, to a rental we were using during our visit "back home."

There are moments, fleeting seconds, when I feel sick with regret. *What have I left? How much have I sacrificed?* I could never go back. I don't want to go back. I've tasted the ambrosia of liberation. I've known the freedom of choice. I've been too long away from that suppressed, authoritarian world that represents to so many people love, peace, and order; but for me represents suffocation.

Traveling towards Elkhart, we pass Das Deutch Kase Haus (The German Cheese House) and we watch two nearly adolescent girls load milk cans on a pony-drawn cart.

That is me twelve years before.

Although I'm now part of the outside society, the Amish Society will always be my heritage; white-hot tears of sadness, regret, joy, and gratitude ease down my cheeks.

I will always be an Amish girl.

I will always be my father's German princess.

chapter 1

Two decades ago a war was raging aimlessly somewhere in Asia. The air on college campuses seethed with anti-establishment ill humor. A combination of psychedelic rock and roll, incense, and marijuana covered those campuses like a mushroom. American youth were protesting a government that was in love with war and the metaphors of war.

Those were the things I knew nothing of.

That was a world alien to mine. My nonconformist tendencies extended only to the borders of the large, midwestern Amish farm on which I lived.

That was the only world I knew.

It was my twelfth summer, a time of questioning. My mother, sisters, and I were dressing chickens that had been on the range all spring. While the stench of burnt feathers wafted on the still air, my curiosity concerning our peculiar lifestyle, the Old Order Amish way, resurfaced.

Looking around at my sibling's complacent faces, homespun dresses, and bare feet, I wondered about our differences from the Great Society. Thoughtfully, I fingered the dark chambray dress that hung to my ankles. I tried to imagine it being made of red gingham, like the one I had seen an "outside" girl wear at the country store the week before.

My mother's ethereal face, so intent upon the toils at hand, reflected her tranquility. I longed for some of her quiet to still the confusion in my ever-listening heart.

"Mother, why are we so different? Why can't we wear bright clothes like our neighbors on the 'outside'?" The query, so like the others I frequently made, burst feverishly from my restless lips.

Mother looked up, the soft lines of her youthful face troubled, and quickly averted her eyes. "Rachel, you ask too many questions." After a long pause, she commented decorously, "God wants us to live this way."

Again silence.

"Mother, do people on the outside have a separate God?"

"Rachel, please. Finish your work. We have no time for discussion. Remember, Aunt Leah is coming to visit and she will be here soon."

A rush of joy swept through me. Aunt Leah! She was my mother's youngest sister from the northern part of the state.

It was a liberal Amish community, allowing women to work outside the home. It was even deemed proper for members to wear brightly colored apparel!

We had spent all day preparing for her arrival. The handsome homestead near Berne, Indiana, was always well kept, but that afternoon especially so, with the lawns all freshly trimmed.

"The last one!" Dear Marietta. I smiled at her satisfied utterance, her simple, freckled face bathed in unadulterated relief as she dropped the last ill-fated fowl in the pail of icy spring water. She was the sister just younger than me. I was the eldest daughter in a family of seven, my brother Emmanuel being one year my senior.

At that moment, my father came walking along the path by the barn that led to the bean fields by the river. As always, my heart swelled with pride at the sight of his noble bearing and purposeful stride. I marveled at his grace and style. He also possessed a brilliance of mind, a cultivated awareness that few men do. As he drew closer, I admired his aristocratic forehead, aquiline nose, and firm mouth.

"Where is Emmanuel?" I was abruptly brought out of my musings by Mother's offhand query. As Father sank gratefully onto the bench under one of the pines surrounding the house, I tried as unobtrusively as possible to start toward the direction of the barn.

"Oh, he is probably still in the bean fields," I said as nonchalantly as possible.

My father watched me, his compelling eyes puzzled.

Oh God! I knew where Emmanuel was. A few months before, he had acquired a guitar from an outside neighbor boy. He kept it hidden in a burlap bag in the haymow; and when the opportunity arose, he would hide away in the dusty hay and practice playing the guitar. With rapid skill, he taught himself the most intricate melodies.

Breathless with haste, I raced through the cow stable and up the ladder leading to the loft. Peering through the dusky half-light, dotted with sunbeams from cracks in the barn walls, I saw Emmanuel sitting on a pile of hay, bent over his guitar, the chiseled lines of his face luminous with concentration.

"Emmanuel!" I gasped. "Put that away. Quick. Father has come in from the fields!"

Frustration replaced the pleasure on his poignant face as he hastily fumbled with the burlap bag. Before he could restore the instrument to its hiding place, Father's deep, cultured tones boomed from the opening of the haymow.

"What are you doing with that?" Father asked.

Emmanuel looked up quickly, dismay etching his face into a stony mask. His voice was apparently frozen in his throat; there was no answer forthcoming.

"Bring that here, Emmanuel." Father's voice was curiously heavy with dread, as though he faced with the greatest difficulty the task that lay before him.

Emmanuel and I slowly descended the ladder, Emmanuel's face pale, me shaking with regret that our secret had been discovered.

Father waited for us below, his face impassive. Reluctantly, he took the guitar and smashed it to splinters over the cow stanchion. Tonelessly he informed us, "I had to do that. These things cause vanity in men."

I couldn't cry. Great waves of nausea rushed over me. "Oh, Father, how could you?" My voice was tight with bitterness. The nausea that was welling up in my throat overtook me, and I vomited wretchedly all over the wooden slat floor of the cow barn. I cringed at the look of numb pain on my brother's face. Emmanuel and I embraced wordlessly as Father left, his shoulders drooping.

Assuredly, the poignant pain of those moments haunts me even now. But, interwoven into the fabric of the lazy, sun-drenched summers and snow-swept winters are memories not only of regret, but also of affection and simple delight. Like mists, they float around my heart, abundant with iridescent color and emotion.

Unconditionally, perhaps mechanically, my father and his father before him had accepted the pretentiously unpretentious doctrine of the Amish life. They devotedly upheld the intangible adversity toward change intrinsic of the Great Society. Their reward was the approval of their people.

It was I, with my "meaningless, illogical, and impractical" desires who brought myself to the "regretful incidents" of my life. My father's greatest wish was that I become a sequel to him as he had to his father before him.

Nonetheless, my nonconformist behavior never mellowed; in fact, it became more pronounced with each passing year.

With fondness, I remember the blissful swim outings in the muddy river, "Old Blue," inaccurately named as it was. One summer particularly comes to mind, the time I befriended a snapping turtle, Abigail. I loved her spirit and would watch her for hours and talk to her while Emmanuel fished for bluegill. Sometimes, I would even go swimming with her. That was certainly preferable to observing Emmanuel force squirming earthworms to certain deaths on hooks. What a waste of a perfectly good life it was; he never caught any fish.

Abigail met with a cruel, lamentable fate. One night, when the rains had swollen the river to a raging boil, she was slammed mercilessly against a piece of driftwood. She was lying belly up on shore the next morning. Sorely grieved at the loss, I wondered if God meant that to happen–to punish me for admiring Abigail's aggressive spirit.

Further reflection brings me the time when our neighbor's barn burned to the ground. Included in the tragedy were the losses of his hay, grain, and two dairy cows. Early in the morning after the fire, Emmanuel and I went over to inspect the smoky debris. The air was stifling, reeking with the stench of smoldering wood. David Troyer stood by the remains of his barn and shook his head mournfully. His straw hat was pulled low on his brow; wisps of greasy hair stuck out from under it. Weariness etched his face and bloodshot eyes.

"The girls should never have burned leaves so close to the barn," he lamented.

Emmanuel and I stood quietly by and gazed with blood-thirsty fascination at the charred carcasses of the cattle.

Dan Miller, another neighboring farmer, tried to comfort Mr. Troyer by saying solemnly, "It must have been God's will."

I trembled with outrage. *God's will! Why would He, who is supposed to be a loving God, inflict so much pain on one of His own?*

Emmanuel must have sensed my anger. He gripped my arm and said, "Come, let's go do the milking."

"Why do people blame these unfortunate happenings on God?" I gazed at Emmanuel as we hurried home, hoping he could explain.

The following day, families came from every corner of the community to assist the Troyer's in the construction of the new barn. The men and boys came laden with tools of every kind, some crude and some surprisingly modern. The women and girls came with endless pots and dishes of food, ample sustenance for the appetites of hungry, working men. Sausages, chicken, potatoes, noodles, salads, and mounds of yeast breads made up the fare. An area Amish man, who owned a sawmill, provided the lumber. By early afternoon, the frame of the barn began taking shape.

Not wanting to miss any of the exhilaration of seeing the rebirth of a barn, I was out among the men, reveling in the purposeful activity of the barn raising. Climbing onto a pile of lumber, I suddenly felt a stinging pain in the calf of one leg. My dress had slipped up and exposed bare flesh, and an ugly splinter was now imbedded in the tender, white skin.

I inspected the wound carefully, wincing as I attempted to pull it out. Quickly, I looked around for Emmanuel only to find Dan, the pessimistic Amish man, watching me in my dilemma with wry humor. Sawdust spotted his beard, which flowed halfway to his ample stomach. He pulled the splinter out and firmly admonished me, "If you were in the house where you belong, such things as this splinter wouldn't happen."

Grievously burdened with humiliation and wounded

pride, I replied without hesitance, "They are in there talking about what is the best way to make lye soap and when the next quilting is to be held. I would rather be out here."

Visibly taken aback by my response, he spoke sternly, "Someone must break your haughty spirit."

Not realizing that Father had been watching the exchange, I was startled at the sound of his voice. With a mixture of pride and embarrassment, he spoke up in my defense. "No one will ever break her spirit, Dan. My German princess is as wild as a mink. She has a rare strength deep in her soul, a gift of God."

I gazed at Father with astonishment and gratitude. At times he was truly a contradiction.

"A gift of the devil is more likely," muttered Dan as he walked away.

Father and Dan rarely agreed on anything. My heart nearly burst as Father smiled a conspiratory smile at me.

By nightfall, the barn was nearly finished. Emmanuel, Hannah (my sister just younger than Marietta), and I trudged slowly homeward, our footsteps lagging with exhaustion. Hannah was shy, withdrawn child with haunted eyes who never said much. But just underneath that timid exterior was a spirited girl that was not so different from me.

"Mother said tomorrow you should stay inside and help with the meal," she now said softly in her childish tone.

"Oh, yes, the men are all making fun of you," Emmanuel added, not in reproach, but out of concern.

I smiled nonchalantly in reply.

My parents must have thought me a troublesome, perilous child, with my smoldering attitude and antics—the operative word being "attitude," because those tendencies were more often manifested in opinion than in action. Inexplicably, however, I knew Father harbored an unwavering admiration for my volatile spirit and insistent eccentricity.

One evening, after all traces of the meal had been cleared away, I slipped off to the porch bordering one side of the house. It was long and narrow, complete with an oak swing. Pensively, I sat on the wooden step and gazed across the moonbeam-flooded lawn where my father sat moments before his discovery of Emmanuel's guitar.

Unlike most members of my culture, darkness never frightened me; and I especially loved moonlight. Unconsciously brushing my fingers across the splintery step, I stared, mesmerized, at the familiar surroundings, now transformed into an extraordinary dream world. My apple tree guarded the orchard, standing in gnarled, contented silence; its leaves now like sparkling rubies.

"Rachel," Father's voice floated quietly from the front door.

I looked up quickly and smiled.

"Are you worshipping the evening air?" he asked as he sat down beside me and returned my smile. For a long while we sat listening to eerie, muffled night sounds.

"You know," Father began in his story-time voice, "in ancient Greece, beautiful young maidens like you were sacrificed to the moon. Of course, they were a heathen nation."

How terrible! I thought.

"Those people were ignorant in their blind devotion to a nonexistent god," he continued.

"Perhaps it was the only way they knew of to pray," I said hesitantly.

Father shifted uncomfortably on the step, as though he knew instinctively the questions that raged within me. *Weren't we, the Amish youth, sacrificed to the Elders? They were blindly devoted to keeping the ways of the forefathers alive, were they not?*

Suddenly I realized there was blood dripping from my hand. I had unknowingly brushed the step so hard, I had punctured the skin on one of my fingers.

Father stroked his beard thoughtfully then spoke, his words distinct and measured, "When I was your age, I asked the same questions you do. I was full of youthful ideals and dreams. But as I grew older and wiser, I realized that there is a security in faith in the Elders' teachings. I found it was better to honor their wishes and gain the respect of my people. God blesses us for that."

He spoke with forced attention, as though through years of repetition he had convinced himself that those were his beliefs. Anyone else would have trusted his seemingly firm statement, but not I. In his eyes there still remained some of the questions of his youth.

"Let's play a game of chess, little one," he suggested.

While Father went in to get the chessboard, I settled down on the swing. Inside, the house was completely still with the comforting flow of the kerosene lamps casting their mellow rays from various windows. In a few moments Father returned, placed the hand-carved chessboard on the swing beside me, and arranged the chessmen on their court.

And so, on that magical night, through the witching hour,

we played chess. When the moonlight began to wane, Father thought it better to turn in. He conceded the victory of the last game. "Checkmate," I said as I made the last move. We both knew he had sacrificed the last game for me.

Joseph

After the chess match, Joseph Streiker sat for hours on the porch, swinging gently back and forth. Mulling over the events of the summer brought back vivid memories of his own youth and the rebellion he spoke of to Rachel, his eldest daughter.

He was, once again, eighteen years old and ecstatic over his purchase of a guitar at a music store in Berne.

He had worked with a contractor that summer and saved enough money to buy the wonderful instrument. He could scarcely wait to tell the lovely Wickey girl he was dating, his darling Sarah, about it.

After the next Sunday services, he asked Sarah to come home with him. He took her directly upstairs to his room and instructed her to sit in the cane chair by the window (handwoven by his grandfather).

How lovely she was; dark hair pulled away under her covering, revealing a perfectly structured, olive-skinned face. True Swiss blood. Expectantly, she watched as Joseph prepared to reveal the "surprise" to her. Leaning into the featherbed, he bent down and pulled the guitar out from underneath.

Her black eyes sparkled at the finely crafted "music box."

"Oh my," she spoke breathlessly. "Can you play that?" After a short pause, she added, "Won't you get in trouble if your parents find out?"

Apparently they did. A few weeks later, just as Joseph had mastered "Wildwood Flower," his father took him upstairs one night after the chores were finished; without a word, he took the guitar from its hiding place and smashed it to bits over the rail of the four-poster bed.

A month later, after careful planning, Joseph "ran away from home." He rode a Greyhound bus to Indianapolis where he secured employment at a large regional hospital as an orderly.

After eighteen months of working nights and attending classes in drafting and architecture during the day, he could stand it no longer. He had to go back for Sarah. He made the mistake of going home to visit his parents.

The theatrics his mother went into when she saw her eldest son in "worldly" clothes were extensive and brutal. She wept in loud, wailing cries then spoke vehemently, "I would rather see you dead than like this." She pulled her bonnet tightly around her face and prayed audibly for God to bring her son back from his wicked ways.

He came back to his family and the Amish church shortly thereafter.

Breaking out of his wistful, painful reverie, Joseph rose from the swing and went inside to his beautiful, sleeping Sarah.

chapter 2

During my thirteenth summer, my rebellion was mirrored in my father's youngest sister, Naomi. Within a week, church services would be held in our home and the bustle of preparation filled our house. In keeping with the custom of the Amish church, our family took its turn in hosting the congregation for prayer meeting.

Female members of the community would gather in the home where services would be held and assist with the lawn, garden, and house cleaning. Aunt Naomi came on Thursday to wash the windows. She scrubbed each pane with vinegar and rainwater then painstakingly dried them with newspaper. Standing for a moment, I watched as she intently polished the glass free of any possible streak. She was not being her usual talkative self.

"Rachel," Mother's sedate voice broke into my thoughts. "Why don't you and Marietta finish raking the lawn?"

We had been at it all morning, and Marietta's serious face was showing lines of weariness. As we gathered the rakes from the woodshed, I noticed Emmanuel in the limbs of my apple tree, pruning branches. I wished I could speak with him; I was worried about Aunt Naomi.

After about an hour of raking, I thought it best that we rest a bit. Marietta sat on the grass, and I headed toward the orchard.

"Emmanuel," I called up through the branches as I reached the sprawling base of the tree, "would you please come down for a moment?"

He shifted his position and kept pruning. "Father said I should get this finished today, and I don't feel like quitting and getting in trouble."

"Emmanuel, listen, Father isn't at home and you can be back out here before he returns."

Reluctantly, he made his way out of the branches and dropped down beside me. "Come on, let's go. I don't know what you're up to, but let's get it over with."

Once inside the back entrance, we tiptoed to the door that led into the kitchen. We could hear Naomi's soft, well-modulated tones now laced with unnecessary remorse. Peering around the corner, we saw Mother at the oak table, her hands immobile in the bread dough she had been kneading, face pale, eyes wide with disbelieving horror. She was so mesmerized with Aunt Naomi's revelation she didn't notice Emmanuel and I.

"You can't mean what you're saying." Mother's voice was shaking.

"Yes, Sarah. Marvin, the girls, and I are leaving the Church." Naomi looked relieved, the worried lines dissolving from her lovely face. She seemed disburdened, somehow; but a sizable amount of apprehension remained. The paper she had been using to polish windows was now in tiny shreds on the hardwood floor. I felt a helpless longing to comfort her.

"Do you feel right about committing this terrible sin?" Mother asked heavily. "You're breaking a promise you made to God."

Naomi was obviously drained and made no effort to explain herself. She went to the front room where Hannah had been entertaining her three small daughters with rag dolls and a tea party, gathered them together, and left on her pony carriage before Father came home.

That evening after a hushed, serious discussion in the front room, Father decided that he and Mother, together with grandparents Streiker, would attempt to dissuade Naomi and her husband from committing the unforgivable sin—leaving the church.

As we supped on the potato soup I had prepared, my eyes often met Emmanuel's and I longed to ask his opinion of all that had transpired that day with Naomi. However, we were in charge of our siblings while Father and Mother were on their mission, so opportunity to discuss it never arose.

We were sleeping when our parents returned. Apparently, the mission had not been successful because a few weeks later,

Naomi and her family left the culture, moved to another state, and were excommunicated from the Amish church. They did not attend services at our house that Sunday. A shame, I thought, after Naomi so faithfully helped prepare for them.

Grandfather Streiker told his daughter and her husband not to come home ever again, and Naomi wasn't mentioned anymore.

Classes were once again in session in the red brick, one-room schoolhouse. Many of the children would walk to school, while others rode horses and still others would ride in pony carriages. We rode to school with our Catholic teacher.

Mrs. Wellman drove a decrepit Holiday Rambler; but we thought of it as no less than Cinderella's coach, so privileged did we feel to ride in an automobile.

Frequently, she brought me books that Father thought were much too advanced. Especially dear to me was a book of Robert Frost's poetry. I must have read each piece a hundred times. And then there was a lovely saga of an Ozark schoolteacher called Christy.

Father wanted us to read books written in German. Such staunch, upright essays they were. He often said, "If you read a book to which there is no moral, it is not worth reading." Much to his regret, that did not keep me from reading juvenile stories that I smuggled in from the outside, such as "Nancy Drew."

One morning when the air was heavy with the promise of snow, I ran down the stone path that led to the outhouse behind the school. That's when I saw the blood. I had not the faintest idea what was happening and was overcome with a sensation of helplessness and fear. Mother's prophecy was surely coming to pass; I was being punished for my ever-questioning, persistent spirit. Sitting down on the cold, wooden seat, I began to cry wretchedly. That is where Mrs. Wellman found me.

After a few moments of inquiry, an understanding light dawned in her eyes. "This happens to every girl your age. You have done nothing wrong," she said softly. "This is called menstruation. I like to think of it as reaching womanhood."

I loved the poetic sound of those words. Finally, I stood up and fidgeted with my homespun dress. "Really?" I smiled up at her, the recent tears now drying rapidly on my cheeks and lashes. She reached into her mammoth handbag, obtained a form of protection, and explained to me how to wear it.

"Do you think Mother has some of these, too?" I inquired shyly.

Mrs. Wellman smiled. "I don't doubt she does, honey. She hasn't had all you children without knowing what a monthly is."

I wasn't sure how menstruation could tie in with all of us.

That evening while Mother was out feeding the chickens, I searched through her closet until I found a discreet blue box with "Kotex" written on it.

I never told Mother. She never found out when her eldest daughter reached womanhood.

Although I found learning an enchanting experience, I often felt alienated from the other students. Many times they made fun of my eccentric ways. It didn't matter, though.

School was a place of learning, of fantasy, where I let my imagination soar to far-off places—away from fractious, jeering classmates.

However, while I withstood my classmates' mockery of me, I couldn't bear for anyone to torment Emmanuel. There was an exceptionally obnoxious bully in school named Moses. The courage he had was derived only from his superior size; he had the brains of a cucumber.

One luminously cold day, he once again began to pick on Emmanuel. I had just come in from playing kickball when I saw them. Moses had Emmanuel backed into a corner and was shaking a fist into his face, while his other hand was gripped tightly around his neck.

"You probably think your father has more land and livestock than mine, don't you?" Moses shouted in discordant, guttural German. "Is that why you have such uppity manners?" His fist inched closer to my brother's panic-stricken face. "Well, I'll teach you something about manners!"

Oh, I suppose you will, Moses, I thought. He who was uncommonly vulgar, with the approximate intelligence and sensitivity of a slug. He who ate his lunch all hunched over, with both elbows on the table, shoving in liverwurst sandwiches as rapidly as possible.

The air was tense. A few other students were gathered around, agape with savage anticipation.

Smack! Emmanuel's nose began oozing blood. Enough already! Mad with rage, I raced through the classroom—between the rows of seedy, old desks, scattering papers, books, and pencils in my haste. Wildly, I began kicking, biting, hissing, scratching, and pulling Moses' greasy hair out by the handful. Truly, he had brought a hornet's nest down about his ears!

When I finally came to my senses, Moses simply stood before me, not moving a muscle, with drops of blood oozing from the wicked bruises on his face. At that moment the teacher walked in (not Mrs. Wellman, but a substitute since Mrs. Wellman was ill).

Moses began to cry. "Look what she did to me! She is a wildcat!"

I spit in his face and smiled in triumph at Emmanuel. The teacher grabbed my quivering forearm and marched me to my desk. "You may spend the rest of the day here," she stated firmly.

I didn't attempt to defend myself; my soul was at peace. I had stood up for Emmanuel. In my desk were my textbooks, islands of treasure where I could seclude myself into my own fantasy world.

Emmanuel watched me with absolute devotion.

Moses walked by me on his way out to lick his wounds. He had a sheepish, beaten look on his face.

"Don't ever lay a finger on my brother again," I hissed. And he never did.

chapter 3

The Christmas celebrations of my youth were somber affairs compared to the gala festivities our outside neighbors experienced. However, that never dampened our holiday spirit. The gift-laden Christmas trees of the Great Society were no more enchanting to their children than the kitchen table, overflowing each Christmas morning with oranges, chocolate, nuts, and German pastries, was to us. There were family gatherings, programs at school, and cards to be sent. All too swiftly, the season would pass and we would, once again, be back in class.

Emmanuel was growing tall and proud and resplendently handsome.

Mother was pregnant again, and with little Sarah barely two years old. Marietta's million and one freckles were no longer so noticeable. Hannah was, well, just Hannah; beautiful as ever.

Mother and I were cleaning the *eck shank* (china closet). Carefully, I polished the heirloom dishes. After they had all been placed on the proper shelves, Mother began stringing the curtain that would be hung on the glass doors of the china closet.

"Oh, Mother," I said, "please don't hide our beautiful dishware."

"That's the idea, Rachel, to prevent us from priding ourselves in our earthly possessions. The pride of the eye and the lust of the flesh," Mother stated, "One must constantly guard against it."

"Bulla shiez!" I spoke impulsively.

Mother's hand stung across my mouth. I gasped in surprise and pain. Mother had never struck me; but she was moody lately, what with the coming baby and all. I glanced surreptitiously at her body, the slender lines now bulging at the midriff. A dozen questions flashed through my mind, foremost being, *Mother, how does one become with child?* Of course, I didn't ask; I didn't want to embarrass her.

Mother wasn't alone in her condition, however. The practice of birth control was taboo in our society; hence the occasion of birth was a frequent one in all families. The most popular expectant mother at church was Lizzie Schwartz.

I overheard a conversation in the library at school one day. Several girls were huddled together speaking in hushed tones. "Lizzie is expecting," said one girl in a conspiring whisper, "and they just got married a few months ago. Do you suppose she was pregnant before they were married?"

I was curious. *How could one become pregnant without being married? Didn't the two go together?*

The voice of the informant continued, "And Lizzie is so young—only seventeen. Mother says she's apt to have trouble during birth."

Another girlish tone joined in. "My mother says that Lizzie is showing a lot. That she is further along than a few months. Some say that if you looked really close on her wedding day, you could see she was pregnant."

A week later, Lizzie Schwartz died. A neighbor lady who had come up to borrow a few cups of sugar found her lying face-down on the backyard path leading to the fields, her homespun dress saturated with blood.

The community was in a state of shock, and young Jake nearly lost his mind. Apparently, that morning before Jake went out to begin the spring plowing, Lizzie told him that she was not feeling well. She had likely been on her way out to the fields to seek his aid when she passed out on the pathway and proceeded to hemorrhage to death as her body attempted to rid itself of a six-month-old, dead fetus.

A chilling fear gripped me as I thought of Mother and the child she was carrying. "Oh, God, please watch over Mama," I prayed in silent earnest.

"Mother, if Lizzie would have had a phone, she could have called for help," I commented with great regret.

"Oh no, it was just her time to go, that is all," answered Mother with resignation. "When God sees it fit for someone to die, there is nothing anyone can do."

At the beginning of my fourteenth year, Father informed us that we would soon be moving away from our home in Berne to a new community two hundred miles south. He explained that it was because of a growing rift between him and his parents.

It was common knowledge that for decades the Amish community in Berne contained two groups of churches, both of the Amish persuasion, who didn't associate with one another. My mother's family attended services on one side, while Father's family attended the "right" side.

As the story goes, an Amish man was accused of committing a sin he never confessed to. That was reason enough, apparently, to have him excommunicated from the Old Order, and anyone who associated with him was shunned. My father's family nurtured an intense hatred against this "other" church and admonished my parents not to attend services there.

Because my father was disobedient to their command (we frequently did go to the "disreputable" church), my father's parents were sorely displeased. They advised my father to leave his home community, that being preferable to his continued association with the "wrong" people.

I tearfully informed Mrs. Wellman of our moving plans during the last week of school. That evening, she came to our house and implored my father to let me continue my education wherever we chose to live.

Father solemnly informed her that the community we were moving to was also of the Amish persuasion, and the rules on education would be no different. With feigned conviction he defended the reason for that being so; Amish girls needed no more than eight years of school. The Elders of the church had determined that we didn't learn to be good wives in the classroom anyway.

I was heartsick, but I had already resigned myself to the knowledge that Mrs. Wellman's well-intentioned argument would be in vain.

Early in May, when we were all completely weary of packing, moving day arrived, Father hired a moving company to transport our belongings, while we would ride in a van driven by an "outsider."

We spent the last few hours cleaning and scrubbing, preparing the house for the new Amish family that would soon occupy it. In a daze, I roamed through the empty, sterile rooms, oblivious to the buzz of activity around me. Many of our relatives were there to see us off. Nothing was said about the issue that instigated this move, since both families were present; but the air was thick with tension. I wished everyone would just leave and let us savor these last moments in our childhood home together, alone.

Retreating to my bedroom, I tentatively sat on the peeling windowsill where I had perched on countless nights, watching the moon and reading books by the light of a kerosene lamp, while the house and its occupants slept. I wept blinding tears for the passing of a childhood on this spacious, serene homestead. I wept for Abigail, Emmanuel's guitar, the river, and this room, crude as it was with its plain walls and unvarnished wooden floor. I wept for the fond memories that would haunt me forever.

Descending the stairway, I went outside, eager to visit my favorite haunts one last time. Walking slowly through the milking barn, I reflected on the crisp winter mornings when Emmanuel and I milked the cows, huddled close to their huge bodies for warmth. I touched the stanchion where Emmanuel's guitar had been smashed to bits.

Hearing a movement at the doorway, I turned to see Mother standing there. Brooding shadows darkened on her face as she lowered her regal head. "This is it. I guess we are really going," she said in trembling tones. From the innermost corner of her eyes one tear welled up, then furrowed dismally to her cheeks. She stood in silence, hands hanging limply at her sides, making no move to wipe the wet from her face. Oh, Mother! I wanted to embrace her and share my sadness with her, but I didn't know how.

After Mother left, I went out to the orchard to visit my apple tree. It stood there, unruffled, seemingly oblivious to the tense activity of the homestead. Tenderly fingering its rough bark, I remembered the times I would sit on the grassy earth under its leafy branches to dream, sing, or cry.

"Do you know I'm leaving?" I spoke solemnly. The warm morning breeze filtered through its leaves, and the tree whispered contentedly. "You don't even care," I whispered back. Just before leaving the orchard, I glanced over at the apple tree. Suddenly, it looked sad and haunted. Its leaves seemed to be drooping.

All too soon, it was time to go. The relatives stood around and waved farewell. Aunt Mary tried unsuccessfully to quiet the fussing infant on her hip. Grandmother and Grandfather Streiker were there, forcing smiles and wishing us a safe journey. I wondered if they felt guilt in tearing our family away from our roots. I hoped they did.

Subsequently, that enchanting interlude, the seasons of my youth on the farm in Berne, came to an end.

But the essence, that wonderful, curious, peculiar aura that permeated every fiber of grass and plant that constituted the place of my childhood detached itself and became part of me. I carry it with me always. It is in my heart, forever.

chapter 4

The following month in our new home was the most grueling, most exhausting time we had ever spent. With the help of some Amish carpenters, the barns were built in rapid succession and the house was finished. It stood in white splendor, surrounded by stately oaks and walnuts. The grounds were now smoothed out and freshly seeded. It was truly a palace, with its polished hardwood floors, wainscoting, and pastel walls. The cherry furniture and even Father's cane rocker seemed right at home, complemented by the new surroundings.

The only social contact we had with the other families in the community were the times we attended church services. Subsequently, Mother thought it would be nice to invite some of our new friends over for Sunday dinner as a housewarming. Invitations were sent, and preparations for the Sunday feast began.

One of the families on the list was the Warner family, whose oldest son Alan had befriended Emmanuel.

The excitement of the new home, new friends, and the housewarming, almost, but never completely, alleviated my homesickness for people and places back home. At times I felt a perplexed desperation to cling to someone, to belong somewhere. I felt so misplaced and vulnerable. Never once did I share this feeling with Emmanuel. I didn't want him to think I was weak.

The following Sunday, with the house in perfect order, anticipation rose high as the hour for the guests to arrive drew closer. In due time, horses and carriages came slowly up the driveway, each packed with man and wife and many children.

The hours passed swiftly as everyone feasted on the sumptuous home-cooked meal. Many times I caught Alan watching me. Although he didn't stir up butterflies in my stomach, that he found me interesting enough to watch was tantalizing and warming. I thought he was nice and reasonably handsome, with dark curly hair and deep blue eyes.

Later on, Emmanuel, Alan, and I congregated under the oak tree in the back lawn. The conversation was stilted; we engaged in small talk and exchanged a few pleasantries. All the while, Alan gazed seriously at his shoes. Sensible shoes, they were; proper foot attire for a farm boy. He seemed perpetually embarrassed, as though he found himself unworthy of even the few comments he did offer.

"We have a ball game planned at Simon's Friday evening," he remarked, and then straightened the collar of his shirt self-consciously. "I could come by and you and your sister could ride with me, Emmanuel."

My brother smiled engagingly, pleased with Alan's thoughtfulness. The joy in Emmanuel's poignant face was contagious, and I found myself anticipating the social event with as much eagerness as he.

"Alan is a good friend, isn't he, Rachel?" Emmanuel remarked as we were doing outside chores after the guests had left. His face was creased in anxiety, awaiting my opinion.

"Yes."

"Oh, yes," he answered too brightly. "I think he is our type of person."

I made no further comment, but thought only of the Warners' odious table manners and of the guttural German they spoke.

Father stopped by the wash line the following morning where I was pinning up the usual Monday laundry. The scent of lye soap wafted lazily on the still air, caressing my face and irritating my lungs. I coughed, and Father cleared his throat. "What do you think of the Warner's?" he asked carefully. He knew that I was struggling to adapt to the new community, we had spoken briefly of it a few weeks earlier. "You are growing up, Rachel," he had remarked, "you will find someone to care about, maybe even marry, and build a life with." There were many things I wanted to do at that time, but being betrothed was most certainly not one of them.

"Why don't you ask me what I think of Alan? Isn't that your real concern?" I commented casually as I shook the creases out of the spotlessly white linen.

He fingered his suspenders and gazed solemnly at the virgin grass. "He comes from a good family."

"They are pigs."

His tone became sternly disapproving, "If you have nothing good to say about someone, it is better to say nothing at all."

"What is it I should do, attach myself to a man?"

"It is honorable to be a wife."

Tenaciously searching for words, I frowned in concentration and spoke fervently, "Yes, of course; but I can do more than that. I want to do something that matters." I drew up my shoulders and added with a flourish, "Something splendid!" Gazing earnestly at him, I continued, "You've always told me that I could do anything I wanted to if my desire was great enough."

His eyes held a look of pained premonition and self-reproach. Shaking his head despairingly, he simply walked away.

As I watched his beloved, stately frame with head bent move slowly toward the barn, I whispered tearfully, "I didn't mean to disappoint you."

Friday came damply that week; nonetheless, the ball game was still on. In a community where social activity is so limited, a small issue such as a bit of drizzle certainly wouldn't block our plans.

After considerable negotiation, the boys "permitted" my new friend Esther and I to participate in the game. The other young women remained seated primly on the grass, occasionally snickering behind their hands. Apparently they were appalled by our gregarious behavior–playing softball with the boys, tsk, tsk! However, their contemptuous attitudes were of no consequence. Esther and I had a marvelous time, and a tradition was broken. Despite the girls' earlier resistance, in the following weeks, more and more of them joined in the ballgame festivities.

It was on one such outing that I had the absolute pleasure of meeting Grandma Shelhorn. She was a seventy year-old widow who lived across the street from Simon. Ida, Simon's daughter, suggested one evening, after a game, that we go visit her. Incidentally, Simon was the bishop of the community and loved to preach passionate hell-fire and brimstone sermons at the bi-weekly church services.

From the moment we entered the century-old farmhouse I fell in love with its quaint atmosphere. We came in through the kitchen, which contained a row of early 1900 cupboards, an ancient gas stove, and a table covered with a red-checkered tablecloth.

Mrs. Shelhorn rose from her stuffed rocker in the corner of the sitting room and greeted us with the sweetest smile in the world. Her soft, careworn face was haloed by snow-white hair caught up in a net. She was obviously pleased to see her young Amish visitors. She greeted everyone by name except Emmanuel and I (she knew them from previous visits). When Ida introduced me, Mrs. Shelhorn grasped both my hands in hers and kissed my cheeks.

"Please call me Grandma Shelhorn–everyone else does."
At her invitation we took seats in the large sitting room. It was
charmingly decorated; a multitude of afghans and cushions
were placed artfully over a medley of over-stuffed chairs and
couches. The modern Curtis-Mathes television set contrasted
with the rest of the old-fashioned furnishings in the spacious
room. While my comrades became immediately immersed
in television viewing, I sat at the ottoman at Grandma
Shelhorn's side and watched as she skillfully crocheted a row
of stitches onto the intricate hairpin lace afghan. She smiled
and said, "I always love to see Ida and her brothers. Simon
doesn't much approve of them coming over; he's afraid they'll
watch television."

I glanced over at the boys, Ida, and Esther as they sat
motionless, with their eyes glued to the set.

Grandma laughed. "Oh yes, they *do* watch television. I
only tell Simon they don't to protect the kids!"

I gazed at her in amazement and giggled delightedly.

She scratched her nose and straightened her wire-framed
glasses, then continued, "Sometimes, late at night after
Simon and his wife have retired for the night, Ida and Lester
sneak out of the upstairs window onto the porch roof and
come over to keep my television and I company for hours."

Listening to her story with a growing amusement, I urged
her to tell me more.

She enthralled me with her priceless, ageless wit tempered
with incredible wisdom. "You see, Rachel, I believe that God
created man individually and that everyone should have the
freedom of making a choice."

I was mesmerized. She was saying what was always at the

back of my mind, but could never express. She rocked gently in the overstuffed rocker. "Most of these children will stay with the Amish; many will be content, but even those who aren't will stay, because they know no other life." Her aged eyes deepened as she leaned forward and whispered, "You are different, Rachel. I knew that from the moment I laid eyes on you. You have such a rare quality, such enthusiasm! You listened to every word just now with such passion. You are so young, so beautiful. Grab at life with both hands, my dear; don't waste a moment of it."

She finished her enthusiastic analysis of me with a faraway look in her eyes and these words, "I'll wager you want to do something out of the ordinary, don't you? Something... splendid!"

I laughed shakily. "Am I so transparent?"

"Rachel, I've lived a long time, seventy years this spring."

With a start, I realized my friends were preparing to leave.

Riding home through the warm summer darkness, Alan commented, "You throw a mean softball." Then smilingly added, "Do you want to go again next week?"

"That would be nice," I replied. Perhaps I could see Grandma Shelhorn again.

That summer I saw progressively more of Alan. He never made my heart palpitate, and I didn't see stars; but there was something so...wistful about him. His manner was beseeching somehow, as though I was the one bright spot in his otherwise dismal, suppressed existence.

He was denied so much. ("I can't go on the picnic with

you and your family, Rachel. My father won't let me.")
Frequently, in Alan's presence, Aaron Warner would refer to
his eldest son as "my farm hand," as though he owned him.
Alan carried with him an air of lamentable resignation and
hopeless knowledge that his life would always be controlled
and dominated.

"When can I see you again?" he would always ask
imploringly and with such yearning, I couldn't possibly say
no. I felt this inexplicable, gnawing need to nurture him and
attempted to, at least in some small way, make his life more
agreeable.

Subsequently, we attended weddings, church services,
and dinners together. I eased into pseudo-happiness, finding
security in the monotonous routines that made a mockery
of the discontent that boiled beneath my submissive facade.
I followed the rituals of my people mechanically, without
question and without conviction. My parents were pleased
with my outward change.

"You have become so pleasant, so obedient," Father
happily informed me.

I despised losing my honesty.

That summer, Grandma Shelhorn enlisted my aid in
doing her household chores. With reverence and not a small
amount of covetousness, I polished the ornate china, silver,
and porcelain figurines that were displayed charmingly
throughout her beautiful home. Many times she told me,
"You are the only person who cleans my house just the way I
like it; your mother taught you well."

And then there was the gardening and the lawn to care
for. In reality, there was no lawn, but a proverbial courtyard,

like the ones I had seen pictured in front of medieval castles in my geography book at school. It was indeed an enchanting wonderland of leafy, veining glory, complete with flagstone path and birdbath.

We would toil for hours among the roses without interruption, save for the occasional Amish farmer who would approach the garden gate and humbly request the use of Grandma's telephone. Truly, her study was not unlike a public phone booth for the local Amish.

Grandma would always assure the visitor that it was fine and go back to her flowers. Once she remarked, "As you well know, Rachel, I don't mind at all your people using my phone, but I do so wonder! Why is it that you folks won't have one in your home?"

I gazed at her. "I don't know," I said, appalled that I was forced to give such a dreadfully inadequate response. However unsatisfactory my reply, it was truthful. I really didn't know. No one had yet offered sufficient explanation concerning the evils of owning a telephone.

Even so, uninformed as I was, I decided that it was quite likely all political (survival of the Amish tradition, etc.).

———

Alan invited me to travel with his family to visit relatives one hundred miles south of our community.

I was delighted, yet somewhat hesitant. I scarcely knew Alan's parents and wondered what we would talk about during the journey. Father and Mother thought it was a winning idea; subsequently, the arrangements were made that I would accompany the Warner's on their outing.

The van in which we traveled was crowded and had windows only in front and back. Alan sat beside me and grasped my hand tightly in his perspiring one. His many siblings stared at me with unwavering insistence. They were all dressed in ill-fitting, somber clothing; and not one of them smiled. Alan's mother sat stern faced and silent, occasionally barking orders to the younger children, stringently abdicating any misdemeanors. The children, for the most part, sat perfectly still, not moving an inch (and if they did, they were slapped smartly across the face).

Alan's father sat staring out the only window at the back of the van, his face and body set in permanent lines of overwork and depression.

Small wonder Alan never invited me over to his house.

After about two hours of an almost silent journey, we arrived at a countryside that was obviously a dominant Amish community. We drove slowly on the gravel roads past countless farms. Huge, majestic homesteads they were, with immaculate lawns and immense sprawling barns. The houses were surrounded with whitewashed picket fences; every window was polished to a high shine. In the fields and gardens, there were people busily at work, tilling and harvesting.

Unlike the community where I was born, the Amish church of Alan's family allowed interior decoration. Taking advantage of that one concession, there seemed to be a contest among the housewives how much each could decorate the respective homes. The end results usually ended up being cluttered, over-decorated museums. In fact, most of them actually had separate living quarters, such as their basement or "summer house" where they lived the year around. The main houses were primarily showplaces.

When we arrived at our destination, we were greeted by the grandparents, Alan's uncle, and family. It was an extremely subdued reunion. No one would have ever guessed that it had been months since they had last seen each other. No hugs and kisses, only the exchange of a somber handshake.

Presently, the men seated themselves in cane chairs under the trees shading the lawn; and the women went in to prepare the noon meal, which turned out to be highly unseasoned, almost bland. The meat and potatoes badly needed salt, and the vegetables were cooked to a pulp. I sat beside Alan for the meal, which was unusual, since it was customary for the first table to be only for men and boys. Eyes stared at me from all directions; I began to feel hot with embarrassment. No one spoke to me.

After a silent grace, everyone attacked the food with gusto, and I no longer wondered why Alan's family had such atrocious table manners!

Following lunch, Alan asked his uncles permission to use his horse and carriage to transport us to visit a few of the many relatives. During the course of the afternoon, I met Alan's Aunt Mary. I loved her immediately! She embraced Alan and turned to me with the warmest smile in the world. Speaking gracious words of welcome, she led us into the roomy summer kitchen, decorated with solid wood furniture, braided throw rugs, and ruffled curtains.

After serving us iced tea and homemade oatmeal cookies, she summoned her husband and sons from the barn. I could sense the same warmth in them as in Mary, except they were shyer.

What followed was an ageless "back home" conversation between Alan, his aunt, uncle, and cousins. Presently, it was decided that Alan and I should spend the night. After the cool reception I had received earlier that day at Alan's grandparents, I was delighted not to have to go back.

After the men had gone back outside, Mary took me on a guided tour of her large, lovely home. Unlike the other houses I had seen, this one was tastefully decorated. Later, we sat in the cool, duskiness of the breezeway. I gazed curiously at Mary's radiant, elfin face and spoke hesitantly, "You are so different from the other people down here; in fact, you are different from most Amish people I know."

A subtle shadow crossed her solicitous eyes as she responded, "Yes, I suppose I am at that, but then so are you…different, I mean."

I dwelled for a moment on her comment. "Yes, I am," I replied finally. "There is such an agony in not fitting the mold. I never feel completely accepted by anyone. There is always that sense of not…belonging. You know what I mean?"

Mary smiled. "Yes, I know what you mean. But much more important than fitting a mold is being yourself; just remember that."

That evening turned out to be the most enjoyable time of mine and Alan's courtship. We laughed at silly jokes, played Scrabble, and snacked on homemade cheese, yeast bread, and sparkling apple juice.

The next morning after a breakfast of hot cakes and

sausage, we traveled reluctantly back to Alan's grandparents. Soon the man with the van returned from his overnight stay at a motel. After perfunctory farewells, we piled back in and settled down for the long journey home.

Just as we were pulling away, Alan's father leaned forward and said to the driver, "Stop at the farm down the road a piece on the right. My brother lives there, and he has a calf I want to take home with me." I remembered the homestead we had visited the day before and wondered how the calf would be transported, perhaps in a small cattle trailer.

Upon arrival at the mentioned farm, Alan's father, Aaron, alighted and walked toward the huge cattle barn. After some time had passed (the children were getting fidgety) Aaron and his brother approached the vehicle carrying a squirming burlap bag between them. One of the sons was carrying a tin tub. Soon the back doors of the van were wrenched open, and we were all ordered to sit as close to the front of the van as possible. Aaron placed the tub in the back of the van, and the calf was slammed into it.

I gazed in astonishment at Alan, who was crimson with embarrassment. Deciding that I could ignore the squirming, burlap covered calf; I clasped Alan's hand sympathetically and closed my eyes. Before long, the odor of fresh calf manure wafted around my nostrils. I felt sick.

Suddenly, the engine developed an ominous rattle, and we drove into the nearest service station.

"May I help you?" An attendant approached, smiling into the driver's window. The driver explained the problem, mentioning what he thought was wrong.

After opening the hood and unscrewing a few covers the

attendant announced that the engine needed oil. The driver instructed him to get the oil from the back of the van. I cringed with horror and hoped the doors would be hopelessly stuck. No such luck, however. Seconds later, the doors swung open and the attendant stood–speechless with amazement, staring at the burlap sack, now soaked with the calf's wastes and reeking unbelievably.

My heart was beating wildly; my head was spinning. I wished desperately I would have stayed at home. Except for Alan, the rest of his family didn't seem to find anything amiss with the mode of conveyance for the calf.

The attendant began laughing and called to his fellow workers, "Come here. You gotta see this!"

In due time, we were on our way once again. I can scarcely remember the rest of the journey home. I felt cold, empty, and contemptuous of Alan's insensitive father. Vaguely, I recall them dropping me off and my thanking Alan for inviting me.

As I approached the house, my sisters came running to greet me. Mother stood on the porch, smiling warmly.

"Oh, Rachel." Hannah embraced me. "I'm so glad you're home!"

"So am I." I sighed deeply.

She sniffed at my clothes. "My goodness, you smell like a barn!"

"Yes," I smiled wearily, "I suppose I do."

"Did you have a nice time?" Mother asked.

"Alan's Aunt Mary is very nice," I answered tonelessly, avoiding her curious gaze.

Neither she nor Father asked any details about the trip. I

never told them about the calf that squirmed convulsively in a burlap bag, soaked with manure; that poor calf that rode all the way home in a tin tub. I never divulged the utter humiliation I felt when the service attendant laughed at us.

August came damply that year, but no matter. That was also the month in which brother Joseph was born. He was an incredibly handsome child, aptly named after Father. On the day of his birth, I knew that something momentous was about to happen, a gut feeling, I suppose. Mother slept a lot and was more than happy to leave most household decisions up to me. I glanced with apprehensive frequency at her weary face and swollen body, contemplating on the fate of Lizzie and her unborn child. I prayed earnestly to God for her safety.

"Hello, Rachel, fine day, wouldn't you say?" I looked up from my toils among the cabbages to see Henry lumbering up the driveway. He was our next-door neighbor whose telephone we always used. He was even more destitute than a church mouse and hopelessly overweight. The little cottage in which he lived was held together by filth and dust. He bathed after dark in a tank in his back yard. Smiling toothlessly and rubbing the stubby shadow on his chin, he commented on my weeding. "You're a very good girl, helping around the farm like you do. All your family works so hard. Me, I never believed in working myself to death, especially since I developed back trouble." He spit a stream of tobacco juice on the driveway. "And then, of course, I also have a hernia that causes me a lot of pain."

I continued my cultivating.

"Your Mother's time is very close, isn't it?" he remarked.

"Yes." I wished he wouldn't refresh my thoughts along that line, consequently renewing my worries.

"Your father asked me to take him and your mother to the hospital when the time came." Henry hitched up his ill-fitting trousers. "Of course, I said I would. You folks have been so good to me–keeping my yard trimmed and bringing me home-baked goods.

The thought of Henry's rickety car with its rattly engine and jar of tobacco spit under the front seat made me cringe. My mother was a lady; she should not have to ride in such squalor.

"That's very kind of you," I forced a tiny smile.

"Oh, I've been known to help people a lot," He grinned and lumbered toward the house.

That evening during dinner, Mother abruptly left the table and went into the bedroom. The seat of her dress was soaked. Quickly, I followed and found her sitting on the bed, head bent.

"Rachel, the baby is coming soon. My water broke, and the pains are getting harder. Father went to get Henry."

Dropping down on my knees, I clasped my arms around Mother's swollen body. "Oh, Mother, please don't die."

"Silly girl! What made you say that?" She smoothed my hair with gentle fingers.

"Lizzie died."

"It was just her time to die," she reasoned, then looked up as Father entered the room.

"Henry will be here in a few moments," he announced. His face was pale, but he smiled reassuringly at Mother.

"Rachel, you take care of things while we're gone, will you please?"

I longed to tell Father that I was weary of "taking care of things" and would like to lean on someone just once. Instead, I smiled bravely and promised I would.

After they left, we finished our dinner; and, presently, we tucked the young ones in for the night. I went out to the porch, sat on the same swing we had in Berne, and thought of the night when Father and I played chess till the wee hours and began to cry softly. I scarcely noticed Emmanuel when he came out and sat beside me, glanced at my stricken face, and remained silent. For a long while we swung quietly to and fro. Eventually, it was I who broke the silence. "I feel so lonely, like I'm apart from the rest of the world, I just don't understand it. Father even said that I seemed more content, and I believed him. I thought I was overcoming the dissatisfaction I'd felt forever." I drew a deep, shuddering breath, "But you know, I haven't. I still want to do something splendid!"

Emmanuel watched me closely, his face filled with a mixture of mesmerization and fright.

"Oh, Rachel," he spoke softly, "I'm afraid I don't understand you very well. You have always been so different." He shrugged. "I think everything you do is splendid." With that he stood up and stretched his lanky frame. "I'm going to turn in before you give me a terrible fright."

Shakily, I returned his smile. For hours, I remained on the swing, through the witching hour thinking of chess and doing something splendid.

Presently, I heard the rattle of Henry's decrepit vehicle. Father was coming home!

As he alighted, Father looked at me through the moonlit darkness. He sank wearily down beside me, and his tired face broke into a smile, "I knew you'd wait up for me."

"Father," I tugged his sleeve urgently. "Do I have a new sister, or is it a brother this time?"

His chest puffed out in fatherly pride, "At 1:30 a.m. your mother gave birth to a beautiful boy—Joseph."

"I'm *so* glad it's over!" I wept tears of relief and happiness into my work-roughened hands. "Is Mother O.K.?"

Father rubbed his eyes. "Oh yes, fine. A bit tired, but in excellent health." He gazed in silence into the dusky night. "It's good that the rain stopped just in time for Joseph's birth. I guess God knew we needed moonlight. You know, this night reminds me of the night long ago when we played chess till early morning. Did you think of that, too?"

If he only knew. How endearing that he remembered it as well as I did.

"Yes, I thought of it."

chapter 5

One Thursday afternoon a few weeks after the birth of Joseph, I was doing Grandma Shelhorn's weekly chores. It was mid-morning; the house cleaning was finished and I was in the flower garden, tilling the soil around some late-blooming roses, when a young man came breezing in the drive in an antiquated vehicle, a sad excuse for a car. He brought "*it*" to a screeching halt, upon which the engine clunked to a standstill. He immediately got out and sauntered up to the garden gate, carrying with him a guitar.

Wouldn't Emmanuel love this! I thought. "Mary, Mary, quite contrary, how does your garden grow?" the stranger called out jauntily, laughing infectiously.

"Very well, thank you," I called in reply.

He was wonderful! He had long, curly, sadly unkempt, dark hair, and wore faded denim jeans and a plaid shirt with assorted worn, frazzled spots. The tennis shoes he wore could have been white at one time.

Opening the gate, he came through, introducing himself as he entered. "I'm Mike Byron, Mrs. Shelhorn's youngest, most notorious grandson. Who are you?"

Smiling self-consciously, I arose from my kneeling position and primly straightened my skirt.

"My, must we be so formal?" He smiled easily and leaned on the stem of the expensive guitar he had placed nonchalantly on the garden soil.

"Oh, Michael," cried Grandma's glad voice from the porch, "you've finally come to see me!" Her aged face was creased in youthful joy as she descended the steps and rushed forward in exuberant welcome. "How long can you stay?"

Mike clasped his grandmother in a huge, hearty embrace and laughed tenderly. "A few days, if you like. I'm on my way south."

"If I want you!" Grandma cried questioningly. "Of course, I do!" She turned to me. "This is my favorite grandson."

Mike rolled his eyes and kissed Grandma's hands, then asked in affected, tones, "Who is the beautiful young maiden I found nurturing the roses, Grandmother?"

She came quickly to my side, "This precious girl, she is like my own. She polishes my silver and tends the flowers just right and even listens to my stories about Depression days!"

Mike groaned in mock dismay. "You mean she's subjected to those lengthy essays as well!"

The conversation soon turned to family affairs. I heard bits and pieces of "Susan getting married this summer… John and Karen building a new home…I'll be playing with a band in Bloomington this weekend." I felt like an intruder eavesdropping on the private lives of people I had never met.

Presently, we settled on the swing under the oak tree. I envied the life that Mike and Grandma's conversation revealed. So varied and adventurous or, at least, so it seemed to me.

Suddenly, I felt Mike's intent gaze on me, "You sure are a deep one," he teased gently. "No one has told me your name."

"I'm Rachel."

He shook my hand, "Nice to know you."

"Do you play that?" I pointed at the guitar.

"Yes," He kept watching me and smiled indulgently.

"My brother plays one too," I announced proudly. "In fact, he has it hidden here at Grandma's; and whenever he gets a chance, he comes over and practices." It was true. Recently, he mysteriously obtained another guitar, one even finer than the one Father destroyed.

Mike chortled gleefully, "I sure would like to meet your brother!"

"You would love him."

"Oh, yes, you would," Grandma agreed. "I've never felt one speck of guilt for hiding the guitar for Emmanuel. He is a good boy."

In no time at all, Mike and I were talking like old friends, discussing everything from music to our differences in lifestyle. He seemed enchanted with me, repeatedly expressing fascination with my sheltered life, yet contrasting liberal ideas.

"What made you think so differently from your fellowmen?" he asked.

"I wish I knew."

"You are a strange one." He shook his head slowly, continuing to watch me, his eyes puzzled and…there was something else—admiration, perhaps.

From that day forward, there was an added attraction at Grandma's: the possibility that Mike would stop by, as he frequently did after we met.

He never told me his age, but I guessed him to be around twenty-five. I loved his cavalier spirit. He could only be described as a modern-day drifter, with philosophies that were as bohemian as Mike himself. He understood my ardent longing for freedom and would listen with unprejudiced attention to my ideas and dreams. When our discussions wore thin, he would play songs on his guitar and dedicate lilting melodies to me.

A few times he said, "Perhaps sometime you can visit my family home in Muncie with Grandma. Then you and I could go somewhere. I could show you around town and take you to our horse ranch in the country."

I would always smile gratefully and say, "Yes, that would be wonderful." All the while wondering if it would ever happen.

That winter passed uneventfully. I longed for the sun-drenched days of summer and Mike's return. I spent the long evenings writing laborious, lovesick essays in my journal.

Alan was a frequent visitor in our home. He wasn't Mike, but then, he *was* company. However, my heart was with Mike. Grandma informed me that he had gone out west for a few months. "One can never tell with him—how long he will be gone."

chapter 6

When the first breath of spring touched the earth, Mike returned. It was usual cleaning day at Grandma's when he arrived in his familiar clunker. Not until he embraced me and pinched my cheeks affectionately did I realize how acutely I had missed him. He was wonderfully tanned and glowingly healthy. His dark wavy hair was still too long, and his azure eyes sparkled in his bronzed face. My heart sang with gladness and anticipation. I was dying to hear about his recent travels.

Grandmother Shelhorn's house remained uncleaned on the memorable day of *his* return, but she didn't seem to mind. Her aged, wise face was wreathed in smiles at seeing us so happy together. Mike told me lengthy, fascinating stories about vast stretches of desert, trees as big as a house, and breathtaking sunsets. He described the untarnished beauty of the waterfalls, rivers, and parks. He spoke eloquently of the royal grandeur of the Grand Canyon, I was spellbound, envious of his experience.

Presently, he reached into the front pocket of his blue jeans. Drawing out an exquisitely carved, crystal pendant, he smiled benevolently as he handed it to me. "This is for you."

I turned it over and over in my hand, touching its delicate design reverently. "Oh, Mike," I breathed in an undertone. "Thank you. But what is it?"

He gently took the crystal from my reverent fingers and hung it on its gold chain around my neck.

"I stopped by an Indian reservation one day. I watched an old man polish this. He called it *'Faith, Hope and Love.'* He told me that when one looked deep into the crystal, one would see endless facets, and there were no beginnings and no endings, no limits—like a reflection of our souls. He said that if one would study the facets, one would recognize that, like the crystal, we have no limits; and we have only potential to do great deeds." His luminous blue eyes looked deep into mine, "Do you understand?"

I wasn't sure, but I told him I did and kissed his hand. Mike put an arm around my shoulders and laughed deeply. "You strange, beautiful person."

I didn't want the day to end; but, presently it did and when I returned home, I hid the crystal deep in my dresser drawer under my homemade lingerie.

I was nearing my sixteenth year. Emmanuel had grown into a tall, thin, incredibly handsome young man. He played intense, brooding pieces of music on his guitar, most of which he had written.

Early autumn, Mike returned to Grandma's house. Of course, I was there. It seemed he always came on the days I was there. He hugged me and graciously kissed my hand.

"Next Thursday you are coming with Grandmother to visit my family and me with Charles," he announced in his familiar, self-assured tone.

"Oh?" I looked at him skeptically. "I am?" Then I broke into a broad smile. "I'm so glad you've let me in on my plans." I wondered how I would convince my parents.

Much to my amazement, Father was agreeable to the suggestion. Emmanuel told me in confidence later that he convinced Father to let me go. He stiffened his lean body as I gratefully hugged him (embracing not being a common practice in our culture).

"I'm so happy I can go," I giggled joyously. "Thanks for putting in a good word for me."

Emmanuel scratched his head and nervously cleared his throat. "Oh, by the way, Father doesn't know the real reason for you going to Indianapolis with Grandma Shelhorn. I told him she and her family needed your help making grape jelly."

I gazed at him in puzzlement, "What do you mean?"

"Oh, you know, about seeing Mike a lot."

"Yes?"

"Rachel, please be careful," he admonished softly, then added. "I think Mike likes you too much. He isn't one of us, you know."

I looked forward to the coming Thursday with passionate eagerness.

Charles escorted us to our destination in his sensible station wagon. Until then, I only knew him from the numerous times Grandma made reference of him. He was a World War II veteran with a terse manner of speaking and brusque personality to match. He lived close by and sometimes took Grandma to the grocery store.

When we arrived at the Byron's home, the air was still heavy with the morning's mist. A strange quiet was everywhere in the upper-middle class neighborhood. From a distance came sounds of bustling streets—the muted anger of racing engines, honking horns, and police sirens. How alien it was! I felt as though I were in a glass house looking out, with the sounds of the city coming through, mysterious, ever hurried and always busy.

The glass bubble broke when Mike and his mother came to the front door of the lovely Cape Cod cottage, graciously extending arms of warm welcome. Mike clasped my hands in his and spoke in a smiling half-whisper, "You and I are going to have a wonderful day."

Mike's mother, Iris, was watching us fondly. "Mike talks about you all the time," she said.

I wondered what he said about me. For the first hour I wandered about the manicured lawn and then admired the studied elegance of the spacious house, scarcely aware of Mike beside me acting as my guide. I was enthralled with the coordinated loveliness of the furnishings, the lush plants, and luxurious carpeting. Mike laughed unrestrainedly at my open-mouthed admiration.

"Wait till you see the boat."

"Boat? You mean a real one?"

"Oh, yes, a yacht. We take it down the Ohio River sometimes."

I had no idea what a yacht was, but it sounded impressive. The day was filled with memorable, mythical bits of magic. Mike played beautiful pieces on his myriad of musical instruments and sang songs of enchantment to me.

Mike's father, Bob, and Charles spent most of the day reminiscing about World War II days. Bob's kind, forever-smiling face contrasted sharply with Charles' impassive one. As his deep, infectious voice mingled with Charles' dour, abrupt tones, I thought that perhaps the only way they were alike is that they were both veterans and overweight.

Grandma was as content there working on her needlework as she was at home. She and Iris spent the day in the roomy, sunny kitchen.

Mike took me driving through the city and out to their country ranch early in the afternoon. He spoke fondly of his sisters, nieces, and nephews. At times, I caught him watching me with a strange light in his eyes, which made me feel nervous, and I would babble meaninglessly. He asked me prying questions about my family, my lifestyle, and my future, that for the most part, I skillfully evaded.

As we rode through the quiet countryside, he touched

my chin lightly and smiled winsomely. "What are you thinking?"

I smiled in return as my gaze slid quickly over his ever-present plaid shirt and blue jeans. "I was thinking about my father."

Mike's face took on a thoughtful, unreadable expression. "You hardly ever talk about your family, and when you do it's about your father or Emmanuel."

"Yes, I know."

"Do you have any idea how your voice changes when you talk about your father?"

I fingered the strings of my covering nervously. "He's a very impressive man—frightening, in a way."

"When do I get to meet him?"

"Sometime, maybe," I hedged.

Mike shook his head in frustration.

"You exasperate me," he said with irritation in his voice. "You speak so devotedly about your father, and when I express an interest in meeting him your answer is 'sometime, perhaps.'"

That familiar, dreaded despair rose up in me. I could not tell Mike why he couldn't meet my father, could I? My father didn't know Mike existed.

Shortly we reached the ranch, a great relief to me. The earlier conversation was forgotten. At Mike's suggestion, we decided to go riding. Soon we were on our way, flying with spirited abandon on the strong backs of thoroughbred quarter horses—over hills, through valleys, and into groves of ancient oaks. Mike laughed merrily at me as I rode carelessly with my skirts pulled up precariously around my thighs. The

Alice in Wonderland feeling never left me that day. It was indeed a time for memory making. Pausing once in our ride, I gathered a bouquet of dandelions and presented them to Mike with a curtsy.

Mike laughed appreciatively. "You are a charming little witch, aren't you? I bet you love moonbeams!"

All too soon, the day waned, and in due time we returned to Mike's parents home in the suburbs. I realized that Mike didn't live with his parents and wondered where he stayed or with *whom* he spent his time. Afraid of the answer to the latter query, I simply didn't ask.

Iris and Bob clasped me in a warm embrace as we prepared to leave. Iris smiled graciously, "You are welcome in our home anytime,"

Grandma Shelhorn remarked to me on the way home, "My family simply loves you."

Charles chewed on a cigar stub and said nothing.

A few weeks later, a letter came to Grandma's. She insisted that I read it. It was a commonplace letter, telling of events with the family and happenings on the farm—with the exception of the last paragraph.

"Rachel is a charming person," it read. "It would please us immensely to have her in our family."

With shaking hands, I handed the letter back to Grandma. She remained silent as I smiled weakly, "That is such a nice thing to say."

It was apparent that Mike didn't understand my situation. I hadn't explained the position my church would force me to take in a circumstance such as this. An Amish girl would never be allowed to be romantically involved with an "outsider."

Mike didn't know about Alan either. Perhaps I refrained from telling Mike about what my church and parents expected from me because I was enjoying our relationship too much to want it to end.

––––––––

The crisp scent of snow filled the air. I rarely saw Mike anymore, but the memories of the day at his parents' home remained fresh and lovely. Whenever he stopped at Grandma's I would avoid him. He watched me questioningly, his face bathed in confusion and hurt.

I was seeing Alan routinely and had become passive in my guarded acceptance of a future that was so subtly, *ever* so effectively being molded for me.

So intense and deeply embedded in my character became this sense of having no control, I began to find solace in Alan's infatuation with me. Indeed, he seemed to be in love with me—in lust, at the very least. That was something I had power over. I could, if nothing else, pull *his* strings.

That premise, in fact, was probably what propelled me into the loss of my virginity.

My parents had left for the weekend to attend a funeral of an uncle in Berne. We children remained home to tend the chores. I was given permission to continue with plans to have Alan over for Sunday dinner—in celebration of my sixteenth birthday.

Sunday morning dawned clear and beautiful. I knew instinctively it would be a memorable day. The previous afternoon, the moment my parents departed for Berne, Emmanuel brought his guitar home from Grandma Shelhorn's.

Its ringing tones woke me bright and early. Someone knocked on my bedroom door. It was Marietta clad in her flannel nightgown. Her eyes were shining. "Oh, Rachel, do you hear the beautiful music Emmanuel is making?"

I clasped her shoulders firmly with my hands and shook her slight frame gently. "Marietta," I spoke urgently, "you must never tell Mother and Father about it, do you hear?"

Her dark eyes clouded over; Marietta, as ever, hated to be part of any intrigue, especially against our parents.

She sighed in resignation, "I guess I won't tell, for if I do, I'll have you to deal with."

I smiled at her with easy, but unmistakable aggression, "Yes, you will have me to deal with, my dearest." I gestured for her to enter, "Please come in; you can keep me company while I get dressed." She dropped down on the bed and suddenly sat up again. "Oh yes, Alan is coming for dinner today." She looked at me with excitement and half-suppressed envy, "How does it feel to have a boyfriend?"

"Marietta, he is not really a boyfriend," I spoke defensively.

She remained on the bed, intently watching the strange, yet so familiar expressions that must have flitted across my face. She shook her head in silent resignation. "God only knows where you will end up, Rachel." She got up and smoothed her nightgown. "I suppose I should get dressed also," she remarked as she watched me comb my hair back into its traditional bun in the back of my head. I donned a light green dress of corduroy, one I rarely wore, except when my parents were gone.

"You are so beautiful, Rachel," she said admiringly.

"Perhaps you shouldn't marry Alan. Perhaps you should marry a gentleman."

I laughed, "So Alan is not a gentleman?"

"Oh, you know what I mean," Marietta protested.

"Yes, I know what you mean," I answered, still laughing softly. "Anyway, why should marriage be the only fulfillment?"

Marietta's lightly freckled face looked perplexed, "What do you mean?"

"Never mind," I said as I shoved her out of the room. "Maybe someday you'll understand." I looked at her quizzically, as if I were really seeing her for the first time, then added thoughtfully, "Perhaps you never will understand." Dearest Marietta, at times I envied her complacence.

Shortly, I went down into the kitchen to prepare lunch. Emmanuel was straddled comfortably on a kitchen chair, softly strumming his guitar and humming a Swiss yodel. Humming along, I began cutting up the vegetables I had fetched from the cellar. We would have salad, breaded pork chops, and homemade bread.

Emmanuel looked so happy. I loved to see him that way, with his handsome, sensitive face aglow.

In due time, Alan arrived; and after unhitching his horse, he sauntered casually into the kitchen bringing with him a burst of crisp January air. Fond lights danced in his deep blue eyes as he carefully looked at me. "I like your dress," he said. "Happy birthday."

"Thank you."

He watched me with a disconcerting intensity during lunch. Emmanuel raved about the pork chops.

After the meal, Marietta and I cleared away the dishes. The way Alan looked at me made me feel nervous; and a trembling, unfamiliar feeling gripped my stomach.

"Calm down," I tried to reassure myself as I carefully polished Mother's best china.

Presently, I found him standing close behind me. He had a peculiar excitement deep in his eyes. "Let's go upstairs," he whispered.

Marietta sat at the kitchen table, chin in hands, watching Emmanuel's hands as they moved with amazing speed and dexterity picking out yet another catchy tune.

"Upstairs?" I asked in puzzlement. "You've been upstairs before. I laughed nervously. "What's so exciting about that?"

"Let's go upstairs in your room and lock the door," Alan spoke urgently. "I have something to tell you."

My curiosity was piqued and I glanced guiltily at Emmanuel before I nodded to Alan in consent. "I suppose we could go up," I answered with some hesitance. Marietta and Emmanuel were completely absorbed in the music when Alan and I slipped away up the stairs and down the great hallway to my bedroom. I closed the door firmly behind us and pushed the lock in place.

"Now what is it that you want to tell me?" I demanded curiously. *What if he asks me to marry him,* I thought hysterically. Not daring to meet my eyes, he rubbed his nose and stared at his "Sunday-best" shoes.

"Well," he began stuttering. "William and I had a long talk awhile back." William was married to Alan's oldest sister, Beth Ann, whom I had never met.

"You and William had a talk?" I urged him to finish.

He scuffed his shining shoes on the glistening hardwood floor. "Yes, we discussed a few important things about courtship." He sporadically smoothed his dark curls.

I was watching him, mesmerized. I had a premonition about what all this was leading up to. Suddenly, my lovely bedroom seemed a prison. I felt frightened and confused. Above all, I felt a deep compassion for the desperate yearning in Alan's eyes. I thought since I was responsible for that haunted look, then it should really be me who eased that pain. I cleared my throat and sank down on the bed running trembling fingers over the hand-quilted bedspread.

"What exactly did you discuss?"

Not meeting my eyes, Alan hesitated a moment, then said in a rush and too loudly, "Well, William said that a boy and girl who are seriously involved sometimes lie together in bed. That's okay, and William said that if you have sexual relations, there's no danger of pregnancy if you stop before the stuff comes."

He sat down on the bed beside me and covered my hands with his. "All the other couples do it."

Alan must have sensed my inevitable surrender as he began kissing my neck and hot lips. I felt a momentary distaste. *What am I doing?* I thought dizzily.

What followed was hazy and muddled, and every moment seemed integrated with the next.

Afterwards, a cold, numbness crept over me. I found the whole process disgusting and felt horribly violated.

"If we do this, then we will love each other more," Alan muttered lazily. His arm lay over his eyes, and a satisfied smile spread over his lips as he still lay sprawled out on his back on the bed.

We will? I thought. I donned the green dress, which had moments before been dropped hastily on the floor. The world turned cold, and the room began to spin.

Alan, who still lay sprawled out on the bed, became a voiceless puppet, his smile a sneer. The soft music of Emmanuel's guitar suddenly became strident to my roaring ears. I stood rooted in one spot—my feet primly planted close together, my body rigid. Alan sat up and blinked up at me. A guilty red flush spread over his features, and he quickly looked away.

I opened the door and left my room. Disregarding Emmanuel's questioning look, I floated silently down the wooden staircase, through the kitchen and out the front door. Running desperately through the frigid air, coatless and hatless, I thought only of escape.

The only sounds left in this silent, cold world were the sobs that tore from my throat.

For weeks after the traumatic afternoon with Alan, I wouldn't let him touch me. My beautiful bedroom now seemed ugly—a reminder of the pain in those moments. Alan became impatient with me and more than once remarked, "You know, Rachel, even if you don't like me, you could at least act like you do."

I longed to confide in my father, but was terrified to do so. Somehow, I knew his reaction would be far from reassuring. The thought that I, his "German princess" had disappointed him once again, depressed me beyond belief. I vowed to myself he would never know.

chapter 7

"When the morning was come, all the chief priests and elders of the people took counsel against Jesus to put him to death," Father quoted solemnly from Matthew 27:1 (KJV) in German.

Our family had congregated in the living room on Easter morning and listened attentively while Father read the scriptures.

Previously, whenever I heard the story of the Crucifixion, I had raged inside at the injustice and cruelty of the death of Jesus. But now, I recognized something different about the Easter story.

Across the room, Mother held baby Joseph tenderly to her breast. She had given herself to her family as Jesus had given Himself to the family of God.

We were expecting Alan to share Easter dinner with us. *Perhaps the reason I didn't feel more fondness for Alan was because I wouldn't let myself.*

When Alan arrived that day, he looked at me with amazement as I greeted him more warmly than I ever had before.

Father, who was sitting in the kitchen talking with Mother and I as we put the last minute touches to the meal, watched me in quizzical astonishment as I grasped Alan's hands and warmly kissed his cheeks as he entered the fragrant kitchen. Father was obviously puzzled about what brought on the change of attitude. He would probably never know that the Easter story had awakened this decision in his eldest daughter. I was determined not to be ambivalent and confused anymore. If I had to be a part of this community or a part of Alan for that matter, then I was going to give myself wholeheartedly to that cause.

I thought perhaps that would still the turmoil in my heart.

After the dinner, Alan and I took his carriage and rode for miles on the back roads deep into the hill country south of our home. He seemed radiant at my change of spirit, yet mystified. I didn't try to explain; he would not very likely understand anyway.

The air was gossamer with bird song and budding foliage. The sun had remained hidden, but there was something magical about the mist as it hovered and swayed like cobwebs, memories of the winter past, reluctant to give way to the sun-kissed youth of spring.

After we had driven for many miles, Alan turned into a winding path that led into the deep woods. An enchanting forest it was, doubtless holding ancient secrets in the bark of the many towering trees, monuments of days long gone when young lovers who were now grandparents had entered its shady depths, their loins aching to make love. I smoothed my olive-green dress with trembling fingers, knowing what Alan had in mind. Yet I was, for once, almost at ease. Or so, at least, I had convinced myself.

Alan watched me apprehensively, as if afraid the spell I was under would end without a moments notice.

Finally coming to a stop deep in the forest, I looked around to see we had come to a small clearing; dreamy, dusky light filtered down through the treetops that brushed the heavy sky. Silently, he stepped down onto the damp ground and tied the horse to a nearby tree. Taking a wool blanket from the carriage, he motioned for me to follow him. With an air of resignation, I alighted to the earth beside him and followed him to a small hill in the clearing.

He threw the blanket on the soft earth and smoothed it out and motioned for me to sit down on it.

"Oh, Rachel," he whispered, "you are so beautiful."

I felt scarcely anything stronger than curiosity, wondering, whether the second time would be less painful than the first had been. Blindly, greedily, he pressed his hot lips to mine.

———————

I scarcely remember the ride back to our farm, the aftermath of lovemaking leaving me in a state of shock.

As I alighted from the carriage, Alan grasped my hand gently and said, "I must be going on home now."

"Yes, I know."

"When can I come back?"

"Whenever you like," I assured him, stepping back onto the dewy grass and lifting my hand in farewell.

He waved with the air of a conqueror and urged his horse to a brisk pace down the long driveway.

I watched him until he was out of sight, the sound of the horse's hooves echoing rhythmically through the heavy evening air.

chapter 8

It was early Monday morning and the air felt clean and crisp as it wafted around my face, fragrant with the blossoms of May. I was hanging laundry out to dry which had just been scrubbed in the gasoline-driven wringer Maytag.

I felt faint—and small wonder that was, considering that an hour before I had thrown up my entire breakfast. I recalled the recent episode distastefully, remembering how my body heaved wretchedly in the secrecy of the upstairs bathroom.

In the weeks following I became so thin and emaciated from the routine vomiting, that even my little sister Hannah remarked on it. "Rachel," She touched my arm gently one morning, her soft eyes filled with childish solicitude. "Why, you've become quite bony."

Father's discerning eyes missed nothing, and one morning Mother informed me that he wished for me to see a doctor. "He is very concerned about your waning health," Mother said kindly.

I shrugged indifferently. "Oh, it's likely just a stomach flu I have."

"A stomach flu?" Mother questioned.

"Yes," I replied distastefully. "I've been throwing up every morning for weeks now."

"You have?" An understanding light dawned in Mother's tranquil eyes. She concentrated on the socks she was mending. Clearing her throat self-consciously, she asked, "When was your last period?"

I frowned in concentration, trying hard to remember.

"I really don't know," I answered tentatively.

Mother didn't answer, and later in the morning Father prepared a horse and carriage for us, and soon Mother and I were on our way. Emmanuel and Father were working in the fields, so Marietta stayed with the younger children.

Arriving at the old block building that housed Dr. Worth's office, we tethered the horse to a makeshift post.

The cool tiled, high-ceilinged depths of the waiting room fascinated me immediately. Gingerly, I sat down on one of the musty overstuffed chairs while Mother went up to the receptionist's desk and placed our names on a list.

There was only one other client in the waiting room, an obese woman with scraggly brown hair, chain-smoking cigarettes. I picked up a National Geographic magazine from the solid oak table. Even though the magazine was three years old, I was soon completely engrossed in articles of faraway lands and places. It reminded me of my geography book.

"Rachel Streiker."

A middle-aged nurse in a starched white uniform and pompous nursing cap stood in the doorway that led to the inner office. Her kindly face creased into a warm smile as I nervously put the magazine down on the table. Mother put the letter she had been writing into her handbag.

Suddenly, I felt apprehensive and afraid. I wondered how Dr. Worth would check me. I had never visited a doctor before, except once that my father told me about. When I was two years old I drank some kerosene and had to have my stomach pumped.

The nurse introduced herself as Mary and was very gentle as she led me into a small examining room and instructed me to disrobe and don an ugly, shapeless green gown. Mother stayed out in the chair by the doctor's desk until I had changed, and then she came into the examination room and stood quietly beside me.

Finally, Dr. Worth entered the small cubicle, his craggy face impassive.

He began his assessment of me by checking my ears, eyes, throat, and progressed downward. My cheeks flamed painfully as he prodded my breasts. I hated it all with intense passion, and silently vowed I would never return to this doctor again.

"I'll have to do a pelvic on her," Dr. Worth remarked to my mother. He instructed me how to position myself.

I was mortified. Apparently oblivious to my wretched embarrassment, he questioned Mother on my ailing.

Mother explained to him how I had gotten so thin and always looked fatigued. "She has always been thin, but now she has become little more than a bag of bones and all the energy that seemed so endless is drained from her."

Then Dr. Worth did the exam, I wanted to scream in outrage. Instead, I closed my eyes tightly and clenched my hands into fists.

"Well," Dr. Worth drawled slowly, discarding his rubber gloves into a waste can in the corner. "I think your daughter is pregnant, Mrs. Streiker."

I felt all strength draining from me. I sat up quickly, numbness spreading from my brain into my extremities. "Oh no, it can't be possible."

"No?" Dr. Worth looked at me quizzically. "Then explain your swollen womb." He shrugged. "We'll do a urine test to confirm it, to be positive."

Tears of shock began flowing down my frozen face. I turned to Mother who remained rooted to the same spot.

"Alan lied to me," I said flatly.

"What?" Mother's face was blank.

"Oh God, I'm not old enough to have a baby." I sobbed inconsolably into my thin, shaking fingers.

"It looks like you're going to have one anyway," Dr. Worth inserted.

I can scarcely remember getting dressed. I walked out of the office in a fog and sat down on the step outside the office door and continued to sob tears of agony and defeat.

A passer-by, a woman with two small children, stopped and asked in concerned tones, "Are you ill?"

I only nodded my head in reply.

The ride home was a nightmarish journey. I had never felt so utterly alone and forsaken in my entire life. All the secret dreams and hopes I had for my future seemed hopelessly washed away by harsh reality. What would Father say? Fleeting thoughts raced through the arcades of my befuddled brain. Every essence of control I had over my life was now gone. I knew I would have to marry Alan, a man I didn't love. A fleeting hope welled up inside of me as I thought that perhaps I could convince Father not to make me marry Alan.

When we arrived home, Father and Emmanuel had returned from the fields for lunch. Emmanuel looked curiously at my white face as I descended from the carriage. Saying nothing to either him or Father, I proceeded immediately into the house and up to my bedroom.

For the next few months, time seemed irrelevant. Minutes, hours, and days seemed all melted into one meaningless space. Sounds, people, and everyday happenings seemed muted and strange. I was emotionally numb and could rarely think of anything but the cold, harsh fact of being faced with an unwanted marriage.

And then the baby began to move. What a warm, wonderful, exciting feeling! That mysterious little stranger inside of me was eagerly making himself known. I began calling him Phillip right from the start and talked to him frequently. Then I was by myself doing chores in the barn; and at night when I couldn't sleep, I would confide in that bubbly, assertive little character kicking in my womb. Early on, I decided that my child would have opportunities that I never had. That became my secret, solemn vow.

Alan became a mere shadow in the background, someone I had resigned myself to marrying. Often I would mentally prepare lengthy speeches to present to my father in an earnest plea to not permit this marriage to take place. I still had not the courage to do so and would repeatedly tell myself, "There is still time."

Plans were underway for the wedding. At Sunday services I would sometimes see Mother and Alan's mother in deep conversation, apparently talking about the coming marriage.

Alan rarely expressed any feelings at all about the marriage and coming baby. He watched me with a pleased possessiveness that I rapidly grew to abhor.

And Father. Oh, Father. I knew that he was allowing a union to take place he felt was wrong. If that was true, then he suffered his agony in silence. *If only I can play on his sympathies,* I would think frequently. But I had mistakenly forgotten his inflexible German pride. It would never do for Joseph Streiker to have an illegitimate grandchild, would it?

Emmanuel tried to draw me out of my shell. "You'll be happier with Alan than you think," he'd attempt to reassure me.

And where was God anyway? Oh please, wherever you are, give me strength and wisdom. Somehow, even then in the depths of despair, I knew that God had another plan for me if I would have the courage to follow the instructions. I knew that I would not stay with the Amish always. *Perhaps now He is teaching me about patience,* I would try to console myself. Many times I would search through my German Bible in an attempt to find reasons for the life the Amish led and the life it looked as if I would inevitably have. "Perhaps I could understand it better if I read it in English." Although I spoke fluent German, English was the language I read the most and understood the best. "But we have no Bible written in English," I would remind myself.

Somewhere, I would get a Bible written in English. If I would live this life, I would make every possible attempt to understand it.

That resolution brought new strength and peace to my heart and soul. Pulling myself together, I thought of outside friends I had from whom I could borrow a Bible from. Grandma Shelhorn!

Oh yes! Remembering that day when Emmanuel and I went over a few months before to tell Grandma about the marriage, I shuddered at the thought of the terrible state of mind I was in.

I had sat on the ottoman at Grandma's knees while I painfully and haltingly told her of the latest turn of events in my life. She had looked so immensely sad and her only comment was, "Poor Mike, I wonder what he'll say!"

Later that evening, I took the crystal from its hiding place and held it gently. In its many facets I saw God and love and peace and hope.

"Will you come to the singing tonight?" Emmanuel asked hopefully, his expressive eyes urging me to say yes. My social life, such as it had been, had come to a complete standstill. I never went anywhere, not even to Grandma

Shelhorn's anymore. I had become a recluse since my body was beginning to swell with child.

Emmanuel seemed so sad and forsaken, as if he had lost his last friend. Often he seemed so deep in thought, as if meditating some secret plan of action all his own. He did not confide in me any of his apparent discontent and unhappiness.

"Yes, you should go tonight," Mother's soft voice urged me to accept Emmanuel's idea as she tenderly wiped little Joseph's face. She looked so careworn.

Suddenly, I noticed something different and yet familiar about her as she turned and walked toward the sink in the pantry to rinse out the washrag.

During all this time of painful, selfish introversion, I hadn't noticed that her body was swelling too. She was pregnant again.

Oh, Mother! My heart wept at my own foolish thoughtlessness.

"Rachel," Emmanuel's quiet voice brought me out of my reverie. "Are you going?"

"Oh, yes, I suppose I will." I smiled tenderly at him. Directly, I went up to my bedroom and changed into one of my loosest fitting dresses. I rubbed my stomach gently as I prepared to pin the matching cape on my dress. "We will be wonderful friends," I whispered to him now. "Your name is Phillip. You remember that, okay?" I continued in German. "I will teach you all I know, and you will teach me; and in that way we will grow up and become wise together."

Soon Emmanuel and I were in the carriage and heading down the driveway. Urging the horse onward with one hand on the lines, Emmanuel reached over and covered my hands clasped in my lap. Slowly, he shook his head, a deep sadness creeping over his sensitive face. "I don't know what I'm going to do once you get married and leave." He cleared his throat as if it had become painful to swallow. "I really miss the spirited Rachel you once were." He looked at me earnestly and then smiled, "Father always said your spirit would never be broken." Shrugging, he added, "Somehow, I think he is right."

By now we had reached the intersection of the road our farm was by and the road that went past Grandma Shelhorn's. "Oh, Emmanuel," on impulse I turned to him. "Take me to Grandma Shelhorn's; and then when you go to singing you can tell Alan where I am, and he can come pick me up." I tugged his sleeve, trying to convince him to do as I wished; yet feeling guilty at breaking my promise of going to the singing with him.

Grandma Shelhorn hugged and kissed me with fervent gladness as I entered her comfortable country kitchen. "Please, come into the front room and sit down. We have some catching up to do." She bustled around in her familiar print apron. Such a calming relief it was to be with my old friend again—a balm to the soul.

"My, I haven't seen you in awhile." She clasped me in a second embrace and stood back to look at me. "You certainly don't look pregnant," she continued, her aged eyes concerned.

"How kind of you," I answered sardonically. "I really am pregnant, you know."

It was true though; I was not gaining as a woman who

is carrying a child should. My mother had several times previously mentioned that concern to me. I, on the contrary, felt very self-conscious of the changing shape of my body; and in my mind exaggerated the size of my stomach far more than it really was.

"You must eat more," Grandma admonished me. "You are now eating for two, remember?"

It was true that my appetite hadn't yet returned to its usual presence, and for the first few months I had thrown up what I did eat. Thank God, that had passed.

Grandma Shelhorn settled down on her chair in the corner and picked up her needlework. "Mike came here to see you last Thursday," she said with false nonchalance. "I told him you were getting married soon."

"Oh."

"Yes, he grew quite pale when I told him and left immediately, said he had to go to Bloomington or something like that." I glanced at her only to catch her watching me with eagle-eyed shrewdness. "He seemed quite shaken by the news."

"Oh," I said again weakly. *Oh God, poor Mike.* I wished desperately I could have told him myself.

For the next few hours Grandma and I talked.

"You seem so deep in thought," Grandma remarked.

I had been sitting on the ottoman silently mulling over thoughts of motherhood.

Quickly, I looked up at Grandma, still working on her needlework. "Oh, I was just wondering, what kind of mother do you think I'll be?"

Grandma rubbed her nose thoughtfully.

"Everything you do, you always do with all of your heart," she said softly. "You will be a wonderful mother."

"Oh, I hope so." I sighed. After a pause, I asked, "What kind of a wife do you think I'll be?"

She smiled slowly. "I think you'll be a better mother than a wife."

I nodded. "Yes, I suppose." Absorbing her last observation, my thoughts were swiftly drawn to the approaching wedding day and all the discontent and near panic it aroused in me.

"Oh, Grandma," I grasped her hands in mine. "Could I borrow one of your Bibles?"

An understanding light dawned in Grandma Shelhorn's eyes. "You are trying to understand your people, aren't you?"

I released her hands from mine. "Yes."

"What you must remember, child, is to always be your own person." Her aged eyes stared earnestly into mine.

I only nodded in reply.

Alan came for me all too soon. As we were leaving, Grandma tucked a small, worn black Bible under my arm. Kissing my forehead gently, she said, "Here, dearest child, this is yours to keep."

"What did she give to you?" Alan asked in puzzlement as he helped me into the carriage.

"Oh, just a little something to remember her by." I smiled.

———————————

The Bible that Grandma Shelhorn gave me was a source of great refuge. The formal writing that at first was so mysterious became a familiar friend. The psalms of David became one of my favorite scriptures, his avid prayers for strength, wisdom, and self-improvement soon became a part of me. Often I longed to discuss some of my scriptural findings with Father, but was always afraid of arousing his disapproval at my reading the scriptures in English.

In early September, Mother gave birth to little brother Caleb after a harsh, lengthy labor. Henry had taken her and Father to the hospital as he had when Joseph was born. It seemed ironic that Mother and I had been pregnant at the same time. We had never exchanged notes about our pregnancies. Once when she had caught me talking to "Phillip," she had looked at me askance, "He can't hear you, and how do you know it is a boy?"

"Oh I know he hears me, and his name is Phillip," I said with confidence.

She shook her head slowly as she walked away.

The birth of Caleb seemed to detract from the harsh fact that my wedding day was less than a month away. What a darling baby he was! His soft, cuddly body brought back memories of Joseph in infancy. "Just think," I told Phillip enthusiastically, "you will have an uncle only a few months older than you. What great playmates you will be!" I began to long for the birth of the child in me. Always the persistent thought came to me, *before you have this child, you will be married.* Even when helping with the endless preparations of the wedding, cleaning, guest lists, and invitations, only a small part of me was there, carrying out the duties that were expected of a bride. My soul was numbed by the welcome opiate of denial. The steel wall I had so slowly and yet so surely built around me became impenetrable to everyone but Phillip.

Secretly, I wished many times I could die or that Alan would die so I wouldn't have to marry him. But we both remained very much alive and, subsequently, we were married.

I don't remember much of the wedding day except that it was a somber affair. I wore a dark brown dress, and Alan was donned in a gray suit.

Heads nodded and babies fussed during the two-hour sermon before the exchange of vows. The Bishop read laboriously from Genesis 29, where Jacob set out to look for a wife.

I don't remember saying "I do." Before I knew it, the words were spoken, and without the exchange of rings or even a kiss, Alan and I had become husband and wife.

I do remember the morning after the wedding when Alan and I were preparing to leave for his parents' farm, my new home. My mother and father embraced me. When I tuned to bid farewell to Father, his cheeks were wet.

I gazed out the small back window of the carriage as the horse swiftly pulled us down the long driveway.

When my recent home was out of sight, I turned to Alan and touched his sleeve softly. In a tone, reverent and awed, I remarked, "You know, I've never seen my father cry."

Book Two

"Faith—Are you letting outer appearances, other people's opinions or statistics rule your mind? Your mind is your world."

- Charles Roth
"More Power To You"

chapter 9

Joseph

Joseph and Sarah Streiker could see the change taking place in Rachel. Helplessly, they stood by and watched her face become worn and thin. They couldn't intervene; their society taught them that a wife must be submissive to her husband.

Rachel came home to visit infrequently. She, hugely pregnant, was needed to help around the Warner farm.

Their quarters consisted of a bedroom upstairs. It was a large, former plantation house—large enough to accommodate the Warner's twelve children plus Alan and his bride. Built about a century before of brick (now partially covered with ivy), it was cold and formidable. The white wrought iron that encompassed the balconies spoke of genteel romance and hospitality.

Not so. Seldom did any gaiety ring through the mansion. The interior was somber: hardwood floors, windows to the ceiling covered with brown drapes, and dark wood framework.

Joseph's heart was heavy, but he went about his work of feeding the pigs, birthing the animals, and tending the harvest with a pseudo-positive attitude. "She will adjust," he said to Sarah.

Sarah wanted to rescue her daughter from the bitter, harsh environment she was thrust into. She merely nodded in reluctant agreement. "Of course she will," she spoke vaguely.

Far be it from her to disagree with her husband. Goodness knows submission had been the topic of conversation at Sister Mary's quilting just last week. Joseph had hired Henry to take him and Sarah to Berne visiting.

Sarah spent the day at Mary's along with numerous other female relatives, and before dusk a quilt was completed.

It had been a most enjoyable day, but there was that moment during a heated discussion when Mary said she was quite sick of submitting to her husband because every time she did, she ended up pregnant.

There were some sharp, outraged looks exchanged, a few secretive smiles, but mostly the ladies were silent.

Presently, one of the quilters remarked that in her opinion it was still best for a woman to submit to her husband and church. Why, look what is happening in the outside world. Those women are getting much too bossy.

Everyone nodded in assent and went back to their sewing.

But sometimes Sarah wondered...

chapter 10

Our wedding was just two weeks past and already it was long forgotten. There was much work to be done. In windswept fields everywhere around the community, farmers and their wives and children labored to harvest the corn before the snows came. Roughened hands became sore from shucking, and more than once Amish lads would look enviously across the fence at "outside" farmers, riding in comfort in their great mechanical, motor-powered corn pickers.

The women were not exempt from the labor—frequently working alongside the men and always responsible for the milking and chores.

Children with crimson cheeks and red noses would

return home from school and go directly about their duties: gathering eggs, feeding animals, mucking stalls.

Occasionally, they would stop (but not for long) and sneak frost-bitten fingers into a coat pocket reaching for a quick bite of Amish sugar cookies. (Mother and sisters had likely baked them just that morning, and they were already half gone.) Hardy souls they were, these Amish folk, with strong lungs, healthy hearts, and ravenous appetites.

The Warner household was as diligently at harvest as any around the community. It was serious business, oh yes, business that would be carried out by the sweat of the brow.

My father had hired an "outside" farmer to pick the acres and acres of corn.

Aaron sniffed with disapproval. "We don't need to get a motor picker to harvest our corn; around here we know how to work."

"How long will we have to stay here with your parents?" I queried of Alan one morning. We were getting dressed in our bedroom. Glancing around the cold blue room with its blue linen curtains and sparse furnishings, I thought longingly of the cozy little house I would have.

Alan's face took on that desperate hunted look so characteristic of him. He sat down on the lumpy mattress beside me and proceeded to pull on his worn shoes. "I really don't know," he muttered despondently. He longed for our own home as much as I did. "Dad still needs me here at home too much to let me go."

The door opened unexpectedly, and we looked up at his

sister Katie saying abruptly, "You're both to come down to breakfast right away. Dad says there's lots of work to be done today."

Katie was tall, thin to the point of boniness, simple-minded and bitter natured. She never smiled. She could have been attractive. At fourteen years of age she had known no other life than that of unending hard work. The only interesting break to the routine of drudgery was an infrequent trip to the nearest town and the biweekly attendance of Sunday services. Alan's sister Margaret was painfully shy, and I could not imagine she and Katie indulging in any girlish confidences. Margaret had scarcely spoken to me since I had become part of the household. In fact, she rarely spoke to anyone. I was relieved that Katie, at least, talked to me, however rudely she did so.

Immediately after Katie left, Alan and I descended the back staircase (there were two staircases) into the kitchen to join the family seated around the large rectangular table. Aaron's face was ominous with unspoken disapproval at our late arrival. The table was crowded with Alan's younger brothers and sisters. All pairs of eyes regarded me with suspicion and malice. No doubt, I had been discussed unfavorably just moments before. I felt as though I threatened them in some way. I shrugged mentally as Alan and I sat down at our assigned places and everyone bowed their heads in silent prayer. The meal of fried eggs, toast, cereal, and home-baked sugar cookies lasted a short time as everyone hunched over the table and, with both hands, stuffed their mouths full. I had not yet ceased to be appalled at their table manners. As I gazed in disbelief around the table, I became aware of

Alan's humble, embarrassed gaze on me. Smiling reassuringly at him, I ate my egg and toast.

"Today we are going to help Elaine get ready for church," Alan's mother, Martha, remarked abruptly. "She is so helpless—someone has to help her, or she will surely forget something."

This led the breakfast conversation into an avid discussion of Ray and Elaine Knepp, the Warner's destitute Amish neighbors. Sunday services were planned at the Knepp's home in a few weeks.

"Ray needs to learn how to feed his cows right, and maybe then their milk production would go up," Aaron observed smugly.

"He needs to do something to feed all those hungry mouths," Martha agreed.

"That house is so dirty, I'm surprised they don't have bugs," Katie added.

"They probably do." Martha laughed. "Anyway, I thought maybe we could give them some home-canned goods to serve for church lunch." She ate in silence after that, seemingly embarrassed at her own altruistic insertions, condescending as they were.

Martha appointed me to stay with the "young'uns" while she, Katie, and Margaret assisted Elaine. She decided that I would "make dinner" for the men also.

Fine.

The "young'uns" and I had a quite memorable day. I dug through some of my things, still packed in boxes, and found my old history book. We gazed at pictures of mountains and grass huts and the painted faces of native Indians. I read aloud about the hero of the Civil War, Abraham Lincoln, and how he freed the slaves. The "young'uns" were mesmerized.

And I forgot to cook dinner for the men.

Martha reprimanded me severely when she returned home. "You're as bad as Elaine," she said. "Someone will have to teach you how to work instead of reading to the young'uns."

I was cutting out flannel baby gowns on the table when the children came home from school a few days later. Bursting into the kitchen with tin lunch pails clanging, they proceeded into the dining room where Martha was mending pants. She spent hours at the sewing machine, with an impassive, sour expression. She was always busy working, performing the same duties week after week, year after year. This is what the Amish folk did. They worked. They never discussed a task that needed doing. They simply did it. An undertaking that would occupy the average person for one month, they could do in one day.

There was no such word as feminism in the Amish vocabulary. There were specific functions a woman was expected to perform and she performed: keeping the house, sewing, gardening, processing food, bearing and caring for children, bedding their husbands (with smelly armpits), and bearing more children.

And mostly, they seemed happy doing it.

Little Mattie handed me a note and shyly spoke, "Your sister Hannah gave me this to give to you."

"Thank you." I smiled warmly at her.

With hungry eyes she drank in my smile, lingering for a moment as if savoring that one small bit of affection. Dearest little Mattie. She wore a perpetual look of whimsical apprehension as if overwhelmed by the cold, formal atmosphere she was required to grow up in.

My hands shook as I opened the letter. A letter from home! I hadn't seen my parents for two weeks, and it seemed an eternity. My stomach moved as Phillip kicked inside of me. He must have felt my joy. Sitting heavily on a kitchen chair, I began reading the short note.

"Your Grandpa Streiker is coming down to visit," Mother wrote. "Could you and Alan come to dinner tomorrow night?"

"I'll ask Dad about it," Alan answered my request with minimal conviction as he wearily removed his worn leather shoes. With that, he dropped his head into both hands and sat on the edge of the bed, his shoulders hunched in tired dejection.

Undressing slowly, I gently rubbed my swelling stomach and whispered, "Oh, Phillip, please be born so you can help me be strong."

"What?" Alan looked up, curiosity mingling with pain on his fatigued face.

"Oh, I was just talking to myself," I answered, anxious to keep Phillip's and my rapport a secret.

Our lovemaking that evening was, as usual, rigid and unrelaxed. I had come to know intercourse as a duty, the one thing Alan should not be deprived of, goodness knows, he was denied so much else. I hated the whole process and prayed it would end quickly. Alan performed perfunctorily, with no prelude of foreplay, after which he immediately rolled over on his side and slept deeply. I felt like a piece of meat, but my sympathy overruled any objections I might have voiced about his behavior in bed.

The dinner at my parents didn't happen. Not for Alan and me, at least.

Aaron and Martha had already committed us to another engagement, that being the annual celebration of wheat harvest at the Stutzman's. The Warner's admiration for the Stutzman's equaled their contempt for the Knepp's.

Audrey Stutzman grew the loveliest garden of flowers and vegetables. She knew everything there was to know about processing food and cooking. Additionally, she sewed beautifully, and was in thought and deed completely obedient to her husband and Amish doctrine. And Martha wanted to be just like her. When Audrey planted hybrid Iris bulbs, so did Martha. After Audrey finished a quilt pieced together in cross-stitch, Martha promptly started one, and so on.

It was customary for Amish neighboring farmers to assist each other in the cutting and binding of wheat. At the end of every harvest, the participants would gather at one farmer's home and celebrate by making homemade ice cream and eating it with apple pies.

The women would go to their appointed place, the kitchen, and the men would congregate under the oak trees in the front yard and take turns churning the wooden freezers, occasionally yielding to a youngster's plea for "just a taste."

This activity was accompanied by gossip, agreements, disagreements, and sometimes even quarrels...

"I think it's right that Ben had to make a church confession about going to the horse races," Ivan Stutzman commented.

"So then, Ivan, perhaps you were wrong in racing one of your horses in the same race," this from Ray Knepp.

"I didn't drive my horse in the races, and I wasn't there."

The debate would become heated, and each man would argue his point. And each knew the other was wrong.

Meanwhile, back in the kitchen, the women cut the pies and discussed their children and husbands. Each would readily agree with the other's observations, whatever they were.

At one point Audrey inquired about my family, upon which I informed her that my grandparents were visiting.

"Oh, you should've gone to your parents to visit with them," said Audrey with a sigh.

Aaron and Martha didn't think so.

chapter 11

My hands were freezing, the numbness seeping into the bones and cartilage. It was early in December, and I was hanging out the endless laundry that the Warner family created. Margaret was helping me, wordlessly and with gloomy, rhythmic actions. Her acne-marred face was even emptier than usual. *She really is getting very heavy,* I thought skeptically. She glanced at me, her gaze sliding quickly away as though unwilling for any type of communication to take place between us.

Pinning the last towel on the line, I picked up the cane basket and quickly ran up to the back door. Entering the welcome warmth of the house, I went into the dining room where the wood-burning stove stood and rubbed my rigid hands together over its radiant heat. My hands tingled painfully as they began to thaw.

"You look cold," Alan's mother remarked abruptly as she continued with her inevitable sewing.

You must be joking, I thought.

A draft of cold air swept into the dining room as the kitchen door opened. Moments later, Aaron entered the dining room. Discarding his filth-stiffened knitted cap in the corner, he ran knotted fingers through his equally filthy hair. He ignored me as I stood silently by the stove. His lined face, old beyond its years and usually formidably cold, was, much to my amazement, full of emotion. A look of anguish and torment gripped his features and flames of pain shone from his eyes.

"I have to talk to you," he spoke in cracked, guttural German to Martha.

Martha looked up from her sewing in cool puzzlement. They both glanced at me, a wordless request for me to leave, it seemed. Aaron cleared his throat, but before he could utter a word I went up to our bedroom. I detected something ominous in the air.

Let Margaret hang out the last load of laundry, I thought as I sank down on our bed to rest my aching, swollen body. "Oh, please hurry up and be born," I spoke urgently to the baby. "I'm so tired of being fat."

Murmuring tones drifted up from the dining room. The voices were low and intense, as though discussing something seriously painful. Feeling too tired and ill from the long exposure to the cold to care much about what the conference downstairs was about, I sank deeper into the lumpy bed and covered myself with the hand-quilted bedspread.

For an indefinite period I lay there. Eventually Alan's voice joined Aaron's and Martha's. After a few moments of discussion, footsteps echoed and a door creaked open, then slammed shut.

My feelings of indifference evaporated as curiosity now took precedence. My heart began to feel heavy as I began sensing something intangible and dreadful. Suddenly, I knew there was something terribly wrong.

Gathering myself up, I straightened my rumpled dress and went out into the hallway down the back stairway. The house was ominously quiet with some of the young children sleeping and the rest outside helping with farm chores. In the far recesses of the silent house was one sound—that of a woman sobbing wretched, tormented tears of anguish. I stood for long moments in the center of the kitchen, not knowing whether I should go back upstairs or whether to pursue the reason for this mysterious state of affairs.

Forcing myself to unroot from the spot in the kitchen, I followed the sound of the sobs through the dining room, the front hall, and across to the door that led into the sitting room that housed many family heirlooms and was scarcely ever used. Tentatively, I knocked on the door and immediately the sobs ceased. Quelling the impulse to turn and run, I stood still and watched the doorknob turn and the door open. Looking up slowly as the door hinges creaked, I met Martha's eyes, a look of dread and premature age engraved on her countenance. A premonition of panic came over me with suffocating, sickening force.

Not being able to look at me any longer, Martha gazed purposelessly at the hand graving on the priceless solid oak door that had opened only moments before to reveal her pain. Goodness, I had no idea this woman felt any emotion, much less could cry with such abandon. I envied her that release.

Awkwardly, I cleared my throat, "Is something wrong?"

Appearing to be unable to answer me, Martha remained silent as her tragic eyes moved from the door to the polished hardwood floor.

"Can I help in some way?" I ventured again.

After retaining a tight-lipped silence for a few moments, Martha finally spoke, "No, you can't help."

Oh, don't thank me for offering, I thought wryly.

"Well, I guess I'll leave you alone then," I spoke nervously as I prepared to close the door.

"No, please don't go." I looked up in sheer amazement as Martha's voice took on a pleading tone. Never in my wildest dreams did I ever think I would hear pleading in her voice. "I have to tell you something."

She cleared her throat and awkwardly clasped and unclasped her work-roughened hands. I could do nothing but stand in half-paralyzed fascination, staring down at her flat, wide shoes, worn to the side, and expecting something formidable to come from her thin-lipped mouth.

"Margaret is pregnant," her tortured words came out in a terse, abrupt rush.

So Margaret is pregnant, I thought, *so am I. That seems to be quite the fashion nowadays.* Relief flooded over me. I thought she was going to tell me something terrible.

"Is she going to get married?"

Martha was shaking, "No."

"Oh?" I chewed on a snagged fingernail, sucking the blood from the injured skin. "Who is the father?" With her face and uncomely body, I was surprised Margaret could entice anyone to bed.

Martha sighed heavily and her face became rigid and pale. Huge, quaking sobs shook her abundant frame. "It doesn't matter; she couldn't marry him anyway."

Uncertain of how to proceed, I didn't press her any further. She seemed to have forgotten I was there as she continued to sob uncontrollably into her work-worn apron.

Shrugging, I closed the heavy oak door and went into the dining room, the echoes of Martha's agonized weeping following me.

Poor Martha. Poor Margaret.

I went out to the wash house where Margaret was finishing the laundry, picked up a basket of clothes, and hung them up to freeze-dry.

The milk house was strangely silent that evening. Even Martha's strident voice was still, and for once she didn't criticize me.

By bedtime, I could contain my curiosity no longer. In the privacy of our room, I pressed Alan for an explanation.

"What is going on?" I demanded. "Why is the father of Margaret's baby being kept a secret?"

Alan's body sagged as he sank limply down on the bed. His features froze with unreasonable dread. "So you know about the baby." His statement echoed with sweeping defeat.

I was puzzled at Alan's uncustomary display of concern for Margaret.

"Why can't she marry as you and I did? Who is the baby's father, anyway?"

Alan drew in a shuddering breath.

"I am the father," his tones were lifeless.

For cruel, endless moments, his words echoed through my mind and seized my heart with blinding pain.

Oh God, not this. Please help me.

I welcomed the paralyzing numbness that followed.

"So now what?" My voice was muted and distant as I uttered the nonsensical words.

Alan watched me with a blank expression as I climbed, robot-like, into bed and curled up into a fetal ball around the child in my womb.

In the morning, Martha's glance met mine as I entered the kitchen. The despair I felt was mirrored in her eyes. She cleared her throat as she flipped the eggs.

"You can never tell anyone who the father is."

There was an unmistakable threat in her tone.

Incessantly, I longed to confide in my parents about the incestuous pregnancy. But the opportunity didn't arise, and when it did my courage failed. I was so miserably humiliated and embarrassed; I never knew how to tell them. In the end, I never did; they must have found out in some other way, but they never mentioned it.

The Warners' hate towards me increased with each passing week. It seemed that Aaron and Martha couldn't forgive me for what their son had done to me.

The ivy covering the vast walls of the brick mansion

mocked my circumstance. It was now brown from winter frost and no longer comforting.

Sometimes, when Alan was out working in the fields, I would slip upstairs. The crystal Mike had given to me still had its secret hiding place in my lingerie drawer. I would fondle it lovingly and gaze into its hot, shining depths.

"Help me, God," I would say softly, beseechingly.

chapter 12

Presently, the harvest was finished, and Christmas Day had come and gone. The magic of bygone Christmas holidays had not been present that year. My visits home were so limited that I did not have the opportunity to help with candy making and other Yuletide preparations. The Warner family didn't exchange Christmas gifts; in fact, it seemed a burden to them to have to take off a day to celebrate the Birth of Christ.

We had gone to my parents' for Christmas dinner, much to Alan's mother's dismay. She had pouted all morning during the time we were milking and then at breakfast.

As usual, by the time we had left for my parents' for

Christmas dinner, I had been so traumatized by the scorn from Alan's family for having to "run home to Mother again," I had sobbed all the way home until physically fatigued.

That my eyes had been red and swollen and my voice husky with recent tears could never have escaped my parents' notice. But they made no comment about it.

One day the pains came. It was late January, and the air was so frigid that our breath froze solid as we packed the bacon in preparation for cellar storage. The Warner's had butchered two hogs the day before, and now everyone was involved in processing and preserving the meat.

"I'll take these hams down to the cellar and put sugar cure on them," Martha remarked abruptly.

A kerosene heater burned fitfully in the center of the crudely furnished summer house, desperately trying (and hopelessly failing) to send its rays of warmth around. In this same room the family wash was done weekly. The old Maytag wringer washer and twin tubs had been pushed to one side and covered with burlap for butchering day.

Alan and I worked side-by-side by the ancient nicked and bruised cutting board, cutting huge slabs of bacon into slices while his sisters put it into crocks and covered it with hot lard.

"My back and stomach are cramping terribly," I whispered to Alan urgently.

He looked up at me with unmistakable fear in his eyes, "Do you think you should go inside and lie down?"

Alan's mother had returned to the summer house from

the cellar and was preparing to carry two more hams down to be cured. She cast a fugitive look in our direction as if suspecting something amiss.

She came over to where we stood cutting the bacon and shoved Alan aside. Her impassive features for once looked concerned.

"Has your time come?"

For a moment, my mind was blank. *'Oh, yes! It must be coming!'* I thought, at the same time feeling triumph, fear, despair, and gladness. These emotions and others flashed jauntily through my mind, taunting me of the events that would follow. I remembered the scripture in Revelation 12: 1–2 (KJV), "And she being with child cried, travailing in birth, and pained to be delivered."

Alan pushed the bacon aside, took my arm, and led me out of the summer house and into the welcome warmth of the kitchen.

"Do you think you should go upstairs and lie down?" he repeated his earlier question even more apprehensively now than the first time.

I smiled reassuringly at him. I knew that once again I had to be strong for Alan. In this moment of fear, I could never reveal it; in this moment of panic, I had to be the calming influence.

My seventeenth birthday had only a few weeks passed, and now I was about to bear my first child. Who would have ever thought that to be the fate of Rachel—the child of the wind, her father's daughter…the "German princess," as wild as a mink, "will never be tamed"?

And I knew then, as surely as the air and the wind exist, I would have no other choice but to bear this child.

Great fear gripped me. I wondered why. Was not this as natural as eating? The Amish society, which differed so greatly from other cultures, had this one trait in common with all other civilized societies. The Amish believe that childbirth is a completely dangerous, risky process, inherently painful and terrifying. Talking about it is taboo; and when it is mentioned, one should only speak of it in hushed, mysterious tones. It is as though womankind is presumably doomed to the horrors of childbirth. Basic Christian doctrine is rooted in that. "...in sorrow thou shalt bring forth children; and thy desire shall be thy husband and he shall rule over thee," (Genesis 3:16, KJV). And stereotypes that civilized societies set forth the world over reinforce that concept.

And so there was I, with no basis with which to compare the forthcoming event to other than whispered horror stories I had heard at school, my Mother's reverent silence about the issue, and the ill-fated Lizzie's death. Small wonder that I was terrified. The issue I was so fearfully confronting was not childbirth-—it was *fear*.

It was nearing dark. I had gone upstairs to our bedroom to lie down. Alan had escorted me up to our bedroom and had been sitting with me when Aaron entered a few moments later to inform him that since this was my first child, it would be a long time yet before it was born, so he would have time to help milk.

Alan half-heartedly agreed and then sheepishly asked if that was all right.

"Yes, it's all right." I smiled weakly.

For what seemed like hours, I rested on the lumpy mattress in our bedroom. The pains, gripping my lower back and stomach, were becoming more frequent and intense. I would stuff my face deep into the feather pillow to keep from crying out. I felt so terribly alone, so terribly afraid. Resting between pains, I would close my eyes tightly, and in my imagination would visualize lush, leafy vines growing over the brick wall. I would assure myself that I was inside the wall and nothing could possibly hurt me. The green ivy surely and finally enclosed me in my refuge.

From below drifted the sounds of a busy household. Occasional plaintive cries erupted, swift slaps followed, and then silence and once again the usual humming of activity.

I was dozing between contractions when Alan once more entered the bedroom, looking haggard and drawn. In an irritated rush he asked, "Have you gotten your things together to go to the hospital yet?"

Drowsily I answered, now indifferent with resignation, "No, I really haven't."

He scratched his head in frustration and paced the room furiously, slamming drawers and throwing clothes on the bed, "I suppose you will need a few nightgowns. And where are the gowns you sewed for the baby?"

Awkwardly, I got up from the bed, patted Alan's shoulder, and tried to reassure him, "Calm down. I'll get this together. You go ask the neighbor to take us to the hospital."

"I already asked him," he shouted at me. "Now let's get these things packed."

"Oh," I murmured weakly.

Within minutes we were ready to travel to the hospital ten

miles away. Mr. Phillips, Warner's neighbor, was to transport us there. I felt acutely embarrassed at the thought of riding in a man's car I scarcely knew, mortified at the thought that my contractions might become more severe in his presence.

The Warner family was eating the evening meal when we descended the back stairs into the kitchen. They ignored us as they ravenously consumed the soup, cheese, and eggs.

Mr. Phillips smiled with sympathetic encouragement at me. My face must have been ugly with fatigue and pain.

"So you're going to be a father," Mr. Phillips remarked to Alan teasingly.

The ride to the hospital seemed endless, while in reality it was only twenty minutes. I prayed that the contractions would ease during the ride, so I wouldn't embarrass myself in front of Mr. Phillips.

The hospital with its tiled walls and floors, cold, sterile formality and completely un-homelike atmosphere intimidated me so much my pains stopped for the first hour of my arrival.

A middle-aged nurse with total absence of personality oriented me to the labor room which consisted of a high narrow bed and a dresser upon which sat a fetal monitor. I was at once fascinated and repelled by this alien modern equipment; I touched the controls on the monitor reverently.

"You really should get into this hospital gown before your water breaks," the faceless nurse informed me pompously.

I wanted to stick out my tongue at her. Alan had gone to the admitting office to sign the necessary documents. A few moments later, after I was dressed in the shapeless gown, he returned to the small labor room. He sat gingerly down on the vinyl chair the nurse had abruptly placed at the bedside and then left. I had a feeling she hated mothers and babies.

Those whispered horror stories I had heard in school must've been true, I decided confusedly as I tossed around on the hard, narrow hospital bed. It had been nearly six hours since our arrival and the pains were coming fast and hard, none of them being very effective according to that sour nurse's reports to me after each pelvic check. What a horrid intrusion that was! Memories of the check-up in Dr. Worth's office flooded back.

Alan sat helplessly by. Every time a pain came, I determinedly bit down on my lower lip to keep from crying out.

"You're only dilated three centimeters," the nurse informed me over and over, after each cervical exam.

"Alan," I gasped when she left the room, "could you let Dr. Worth know I'm here. I think something is terribly wrong."

"I'll ask the nurse up at the desk." He went out into the corridor. My back felt as though it were breaking in two, as though the baby's feet were there, pushing with all its tiny might. Moments later, Alan returned with the nurse from the desk. She smiled warmly at me. Oh, how wonderful, someone who knew how to smile!

"I'm Hilda," she spoke warmly. "You're being very brave." Then she added as an afterthought, "The nurse that is caring for you is Hattie. She's never had any children, so sometimes she seems quite unsympathetic."

You could've fooled me, I thought.

"You are dilating very slowly," Hilda informed me as she did the pelvic check, much gentler than Hattie. "Your pelvic structure is quite small and, besides that, I believe that the baby is turned the wrong way. I believe I'll call Dr. Worth."

Relief flooded through me. Surely he would help.

"I want water, please," I begged repeatedly to nameless, faceless nurses whose number had now increased to three. I had become disoriented and semi-conscious with pain. Alan had long disappeared into the men's lounge. "You can only have ice chips," a blurred voice spoke above me. A styrofoam cup was placed in my hands which I promptly flung across the sterile room, livid with anger and irritable with pain. *Damn them, I wanted water, not ice chips!*

"Hattie, stay here while I get fifty milligrams of Demerol for this child. My God, I wish Dr. Worth would get here. We have a breech birth," Hilda muttered under her breath, her voice sounding desperate.

Now they're going to stick you with a needle and some dreadful drugs, a voice inside of me warned.

"No," I screamed, "please don't," when Hilda returned with the syringe. A dozen pair of hands suddenly shot out from nowhere and gripped me as Hilda injected the stinging, potent liquid into my thigh.

The drug I had been given floated me in and out of reality.

Vaguely, I remember Dr. Worth's brutish, bulbous face floating above me, insensitive and unsympathetic. "I'm going to the doctor's lounge and sleep awhile. It will be quite some time before this baby is born."

"But she is not progressing well," Hilda's soft voice filtered through my subconscious. "Perhaps you should consider a c section."

"No," Dr. Worth's voice faded in the distance.

I was sure I was dying. This must be how Lizzie felt. I marveled that my mother had been through this seven times. *My God! I would rather die!*

"If you just let me get up and walk around, this backache will go away," I begged.

No one bothered to answer me. In due time, likely when Dr. Worth thought I had suffered enough, I was wheeled on a trolley into a stainless steel room with stainless steel furniture and was placed on a bed even more narrow and hard than the first one.

My feet and knees were thrust rudely up into stirrup-like structures and quickly strapped in. Screaming, shrieking, and biting any hand or object that came close to my mouth, I attempted to tear out of the straps. Even my wrists were now strapped.

What an unforgivable injustice! They were treating me like an animal. I was sure the whole world had gone berserk, and I likely was half-dead already.

A mask with some horrid smelling odor was clamped over my face, and I lost consciousness.

Unfamiliar sounds hovered in the room, penetrating my still half-drugged brain. A hand shook my shoulder urgently, "Rachel, wake up. Your little boy is hungry."

Opening my eyes slowly, I saw the most beautiful, perfect baby I had ever seen. My son.

"You've been sleeping for five hours," the young, pleasant-faced nurse informed me with a kind smile. Nowhere did I see Hilda or Hattie or the other nurses. They all seemed to be part of a distant horror story I longed to forget, and that even now was fading into oblivion.

I realized that I, as the darling child that now was feeding hungrily at my breast, was ravenous.

I looked around at my pleasant surroundings. I had now been put in a tastefully furnished private room with soft blue walls and curtains. "Oh this is much better than that horrid stainless steel room," I commented happily to my son and caressed his soft cheeks reverently. I touched and checked out every inch of his body, assuring myself that he had the right amount of fingers and toes. Then I noticed the ugly bruises on his left shoulder. I was mortified. I stroked his long, silky dark hair lovingly. "Oh, Phillip," I whispered in shock tones, "what did they do to you?"

"What happened here," I demanded of the young nurse when she returned to take Phillip back to the nursery.

She cleared her throat and shrugged uncomfortably, then remarked with forced casualness, "Those are forceps marks."

"Forceps marks?"

"Yes, the baby came out the wrong way and your pelvic structure was too small to let the baby pass through as normal, so the forceps had to be used."

I was appalled.

"Where is my husband?" I asked as the nurse was leaving with Phillip cuddled in her arms.

"He went home to do chores," the nurse informed me. "He said he'd be back later on this evening."

"May I have something to eat?" I added eagerly as the nurse disappeared through the door into the corridor.

"Just a moment," her pleasant voice drifted back.

After the meal of usual hospital fare, I dropped into a deep, dreamless slumber. I never found out when Alan came in that evening. I could scarcely remember ever feeling so tired.

chapter 13

Alan and his family seemed curiously apathetic towards Phillip.

Our upstairs bedroom was so cold at times during those frigid winter months; I was terrified that my baby would become sick. He remained in good health, however, and with each passing week became more active and curious. He cooed and gurgled and tried to eat his fists and screamed vigorously when he was hungry.

I watched his every movement, and the moment he did something new I would proudly inform Alan's mother and sisters only to have my announcements greeted by sheer boredom.

When Phillip was three weeks old we once more began attending Sunday services. With great pleasure, I dressed Phillip in a soft blue baby gown, a gift from Aunt Leah.

It would be nice to see my parents at Sunday services also. I hadn't seen them but once, when they had come over a few days after I had come back to Warners' with Phillip. They had received such a cold reception from Alan's parents,' they likely wouldn't repeat the visit very soon.

I looked up eagerly as Alan entered the bedroom a few moments later, his face rosy from the cold. "Can we go over to my parents after church?" I asked longingly.

"Yes, I suppose so," he answered softly, and then his face became bitter. "You know we have to be home to help with the milking, or Dad will get real upset."

Phillip squirmed in protest as I wrapped him in the lovely pastel-colored afghan that Grandma Shelhorn had given to me a few months before his birth.

"Mom said you couldn't use that blanket because it wasn't plain," Alan warned me.

"Did she now?" I remarked, cynicism dripping from my voice.

Alan's parents had already left for services when we came downstairs. Margaret, who was now hugely pregnant, was not attending church; and some of the children were staying home with her.

Presently, we arrived at the home where services were being held. Carriages were arriving from every direction, wheels squeaking and crunching over the frozen gravel roads.

Men with wide-rimmed, black hats and boys with hand-knitted caps congregated at random in the barn yard, stomping their feet with cold, their frozen breath wafting heavenward.

Wool coats and insulated boots filled every corner and available surface of the washhouse. Every respectable Amish home had a washhouse. Not only are they a necessity for doing family laundry every Monday, they were frequently utilized for processing food (that kept the mess out of the meticulously clean kitchens) and housing winter wraps during church services.

Curious faces greeted me when I entered the back door of the kitchen a few moments later, girls wearing white capes and aprons, standing at attention like soldiers at Windsor. Mothers clasped their infants and hushed their already quiet youngsters.

Shortly thereafter, my mother and sisters descended upon Phillip, cooing noisily over his infant beauty. "What a lovely blanket!" Mother observed. Her concerned eyes embraced me. "How have you been?" she asked as she retied the strings on her covering.

I watched the girls as they continued to coo over Phillip, oblivious to the puzzled stares they evoked at the ado they were making over my son. Rarely was such emotion displayed, especially in the somberness of a church service.

Mother watched them fondly for a moment then looked back when she realized I hadn't answered her question. "You are doing fine, are you not?"

"Yes," I answered faintly. Once again, I longed to confide in her about the other child that would soon be born.

At nine o'clock, as is conventional at Amish services, the men and boys filed into the big living room, and one by one sat down on the long rows of benches and removed their wide-rimmed black hats. The four ministers went around shaking everyone's hands in greeting and then seated themselves on the four chairs facing the congregation in the living room consisting of mostly men. The women sat on the remaining seats of the living room, and the rest sat in the kitchen and dining area or wherever they could find a seat.

Phillip slept most of the time during the four-hour services, waking up only once to be fed. I held him the entire time, fearful that if I laid him on the bed with the other babies some unspoken harm could befall him. The other mothers glanced at each other, at intervals making remarks to each other behind cupped hands, likely wondering why I never put him down so he could "rest better."

Amish children are absurdly well behaved. Especially so at "Sunday meeting." Fear, awe, and occasional curiosity bathe the innocent faces of the sons and daughters as they inch closer to their parents throughout the lengthy sermon about "our wrathful, jealous God. He wants us to stay close to Him and not follow the ways of the world," the Bishop bellows earnestly to the devout followers. "The fires of hell are waiting for those who fall by the way."

Righteous mothers glance accusingly at the brightly colored blanket wrapped around Phillip's infant body. *Poor innocent child. He can't help what his mother puts around him.*

Other heads about the room bow in shame and guilt, admissions of secret transgression. *How can I pretend to be humble when the color of my dress is much too bright? I must confess about the telephone I had secretly installed in the cattle barn.* Young parents, already blessed with five or six children think remorsefully of the diaphragm hidden in the bedroom closet.

Surely, they must "put away the ways of the world" or they will all be damned.

And the children snuggle closer to their parents, lest some unspoken harm befall them and the devil take them.

Presently, a plate of Amish sugar cookies is passed around and is quickly emptied by the hungry children and, momentarily, the thundering sermon is forgotten. They think of the end of the service when they can go outside and play tag or kickball. But the fear of damnation stays with them for a long time.

After the final, fervent prayer, the men swiftly set up benches on trestles which would serve as tables from which the lunch of cheese, summer sausage, and relish arrangements, would be eaten. Coffee, tea, and water were the beverages. My sisters held Phillip while I ate. Alan's mother didn't speak to me once during the day, and I sensed she was upset that I had wrapped Phillip in Grandma Shelhorn's afghan against her will. I felt no remorse.

The afternoon at my parents' passed all too swiftly as we sang all the old songs again, drank tea, and reminisced about days on the farm in Berne.

Around five o'clock, Alan became restless and I knew he was beginning to worry what his father would say if we didn't return soon.

After many good-byes, and "come back soons" we were on our way back to Alan's parents' farm.

Upon arrival, I quickly went to the house, while Alan

unhitched and stabled the horse. I clasped Phillip tightly to my breast as though he could be a protective shield. When I entered the kitchen through the side door, Margaret was dressing in her over clothes, preparing for evening chores.

Breathless from the dash into the house, I paused a moment in the kitchen to catch my breath.

"Hello, Margaret," I said and smiled at her.

With an effort, she fastened the last hook and eye of her coat over her protruding tummy and looked up, an unbecoming sneer on her face. She ignored my greeting.

The munching of popcorn and occasional scrape of chairs greeted me from the dining room. Stepping forward a bit, I peered into the room to see Aaron, Martha, and the children sitting around in mournful meditation.

Aaron fidgeted with the suspenders that held up his oversized pants. Pompous as a feudal lord, he arose from the rocking chair. Seconds later a gust of cold air announced Alan's entrance.

Aaron cleared his throat, looked in my direction, but refused to meet my eyes. "You're not to use that blanket anymore," he said sternly.

"Oh," my voice was icy.

Martha's guttural voice joined in, "You think you can do just whatever you like, don't you?"

Aaron cleared his throat once more and threw his words at me vengefully, "Your father told me on the day you and Alan were married that we would have to make ourselves 'boss' over you because you never listened to adult advice."

I felt myself go pale with shock. *My father gave him the right to rule over me? How could he?*

"I don't believe you," I heard my voice come from somewhere, remote and feeble.

As Aaron lumbered past me into the kitchen, now satisfied that he had inflicted sufficient pain, I became aware that Alan was standing silently beside me. He took Phillip out of my arms, unwrapped the afghan, and put it on a chair by the dining room table.

"Come, let's go upstairs," he said softly.

Martha picked up the precious afghan, destruction written on her face.

Tearing my arm from Alan's grip, I wretched it from Martha's hands, "No," I screamed. "You can never have this to destroy. It is mine! Mine and Phillips!"

With those words, I grabbed Phillip from Alan's arms, wrapped him in the afghan, and tore up the back stairs, leaving everyone staring after me, aghast at my aggression.

chapter 14

The hint of spring was once more in the air. In barns everywhere on the Warner farm new life was born. Baby calves, piglets, colts, and kittens sprung forth, eager to taste the world outside of the womb. Rains came and went, and the sun shone erratically, coming out from behind restricting clouds at intervals with an air of indignance at not being allowed to shine in her full glory, without interruption.

Margaret, Katie, and I were doing the milking while Alan and his father were off in a barn somewhere else assisting with the birth of yet another calf. Alan's younger brother, Wilbur, had come into the milking barn a few minutes before and informed us nonchalantly that the cow was having difficulty giving birth, so Alan and his father had tied a rope around the calf's protruding front feet and were pulling it out with the rope. I felt nauseous.

Margaret went about her work with an impassive lack of emotion. She seemed even quieter than usual that evening and rarely spoke, even to Katie.

That night her child was born, Martha had abruptly informed Alan and I before we retired that evening that Margaret's pains had begun and she and Aaron had asked the neighbor, Mr. Phillips, to escort them and Margaret to the hospital. Alan said nothing, and his face was expressionless.

We spoke little as we prepared for bed. I dressed Phillip in his nightshirt and changed his diaper, meditating how he would soon have a brother or sister.

Tenderly, I drew him to me as he fed at my breast. After he fell asleep, I placed him in his cradle and patted his back softly as he stirred fitfully.

Alan lay on his side facing the wall and remained silent. I guessed he was sleeping by then.

I gazed at the back of his dark curly head as the kerosene lamp flickered spasmodically and felt curiously empty of emotion.

I went to the floor-length window at one end of the room and stared out over the moonlit fields dotted with occasional shadows that I knew were Aaron's thoroughbred horses. I thought of bygone moonlit nights, nights when fantasy seemed real. Tonight reality seemed the nightmare. Presently, I took the crystal from its hiding place and clasped it tightly in my hands, reveling in the white heat it exuded.

I sighed a trembling sigh, and for what seemed like an

eternity I stood at the window and stared unseeingly at nothing and wished myself into worlds far away, the same worlds that I found refuge in many times in the past.

I don't remember going to bed that night, but eventually morning arrived. Martha remarked to everyone at the breakfast table in the morning that Margaret had a son. No one seemed unduly excited about the news. Alan made no comment as he hastily shoved fried potatoes and eggs into his mouth.

The next afternoon, Margaret came home with her son, whom she named William. He was a beautiful baby, full of health and infant innocence.

That following summer seemed to go on forever. The Warner family's antagonism remained alive and strong and never ebbing. I became indifferent to it.

In due time, Margaret once again began attending Sunday services. Martha cared for baby William as though he was her own, and Margaret would occupy a church bench alongside her peers.

Although there were many whispers behind cupped hands and secretive, knowing looks exchanged, Margaret and her infant were accepted with surprising tolerance by the Amish folk, however hesitant and tempered with pity it may have been.

The times during that summer that I saw my parents, my father spoke to me only when necessary and then with great effort. The dark circles under my eyes spoke plainly of the torment within. He watched me surreptitiously—unvoiced concern written on his face and encompassing his being.

Mother frequently commented, "You're much too thin. You should eat more,"

Then she would heap my plate with yeast bread and mashed potatoes, and instruct me to "finish everything, there are starving children in India."

Food—the Amish remedy for all ills.

"Eat. You will feel better. It will give you strength. Let's not waste anything."

Mother was mild, though, compared to my friend Esther's mother. She spoke of children starving in countries that didn't exist. Hence, there was Esther, the nice, plump, frugal Amish girl.

Mother took my refusal of the generous plate of food as a personal insult.

I didn't want to eat. I wanted to talk, to confide in her about Alan's other child, but my tongue stuck to the roof of my mouth.

She and Father carefully avoided speaking of William, although by now it was common knowledge in the community that Margaret's illegitimate child was fathered by Alan.

I rarely saw Grandma Shelhorn anymore, and when I did it was only for a few moments when I would coerce Alan to stop by on our way to or from my parents' home. She would always embrace me ecstatically, admire Phillip, and feed us gingersnaps and milk. It was that occasional hurried exchange with her that kept my faith and hope alive. She would inform me about Mike's whereabouts and what he was doing as though she knew that I secretly longed to hear about him. Alan usually stayed out on the porch swing while Grandma and I exchanged secrets.

Emmanuel grew progressively more morose that summer. By then he had smuggled his guitar to an old dilapidated barn that stood haphazardly at the back end of my parent's farm. With eyes aglow, he told me that he'd slip back there at night when everyone else was asleep and play music he had written. I prayed fervently that Father wouldn't find the guitar and smash the light out of my brother's day.

chapter 15

Three months after Phillip's first birthday, I realized I was pregnant again. In addition to the absence of my period, I was sick in the mornings again.

Using the Phillips' telephone, I contacted an obstetrician in Shelbyville for my first checkup.

Martha gave Alan a lecture on the dangers of my progressive ideas and how we would never be able to afford the expense of a specialist for all my pregnancies.

What she didn't know was that this would be my last pregnancy for a long time. Dr. Julian had told me about the pill. I thought it was marvelous. Alan would never know. I appreciated that I would have some control of my life.

After the morning sickness subsided, I found that I began to enjoy the pregnancy and began to fantasize about the lovely baby daughter I would have.

Nothing ever changed in the Warner household. Life held the same monotonous pace day after day, month after month. Familiarity was their security. In the same way I craved newness, they clung to old ways. The marks of the most orthodox Amish people are their conformity to routine and their aversion to change.

The Warner's were "good Amish people" because they firmly believed in and practiced the favorite Amish adage: "the new is deceptive and comes from the devil."

The air was oppressive for May. In the same tradition as they had vigorously gathered their autumn bounty, Amish families now took their horse-drawn plows and planters to the fields, tilling, nurturing, feeding, and planting seeds into the warm, welcoming embrace of the fertile earth.

Sweat eased in welcome droplets down my temples and cooled my forehead. The rows of beans seemed to go on forever. Margaret and I were hoeing the weeds in the rows. Later we would hitch a Percheron draft horse to the hand plow and till between the rows. We exchanged no words during our toil. I enjoyed the silence; it was my friend. Margaret never said anything enlightening or intelligent anyway. She didn't like me. I didn't like her; and, quite frankly, it didn't matter.

"Hello," Mattie's quaint face was creased in a cautious smile as she shyly handed me a post card. "This came in the mail for you."

"Thank you, Mattie," I smiled in return, wiping beads of sweat from my forehead.

It was a note from Grandma Shelhorn informing me of a family reunion at her home on Saturday.

"Please, you come also," she wrote. "My family would love to see you and Phillip."

My heart sang, and instantly I thought of Mike. His nonchalant, handsome face filled my mind and memories of past times with him lifted my spirits.

Sinking wearily onto a stump at the edge of the garden, I read the note once more. I fantasized how the meeting between Mike and I would be. My pregnancy was still not noticeable, with only a hint of swelling around my abdomen.

For a moment, I stared unseeingly down at my dusty feet and ran my fingers slowly over the rough bark of the stump. Should I tell Mike that I was pregnant again, or wouldn't he be interested?

My heart quickened as I thought of his gentle voice.

Reprimanding myself for such intimate thoughts, I went back to my toils among the beans with the still silent Margaret.

Glancing apprehensively behind me through the small window in the back of the carriage, I noticed that there were three automobiles following me, afraid to pass because of the hill just ahead. Lightly tapping the driving lines across Ribbon's back, I urged her onward to the top of the hill. I was on my way to Grandma Shelhorn's family reunion. The air was cool with a promise of heat in the early morning sun.

The automobiles passed my carriage one by one and

sped down the narrow highway, impatiently carrying on their business. Phillip watched the cars rush by with curious attentiveness, as though he, as I, wondered where they were all off to.

When I arrived at Grandma Shelhorn's shady farm, everyone, children and adults alike, came running out to greet me, fascinated with the horse and buggy.

"Let us pet the horse," several small children requested hopefully as I alighted. I had driven Ribbon to the fence by the old barn where she would have protection from the sun by the huge old oak trees that were everywhere on Grandma's farm.

"Of course," I smiled at the children, who were likely Mike's nieces and nephews. He was nowhere around, and I felt conflicting relief and disappointment.

After tethering Ribbon securely to the fence, I drew Phillip off the carriage seat and walked toward the house, leaving the children petting Ribbon; the men inspecting the carriage; and Iris, Mike's mother, walking beside me.

"How have you been?" she asked as she motioned for me to hand Phillip to her. She seemed so happy to see me again. I wished I could tell her how I really was.

"I've been fine, how've you been?" I marveled at the emptiness of small talk and sighed with relief for the convenience of it.

Grandma Shelhorn stood at the garden gate, wreathed in smiles, and embraced me.

"Oh, Rachel, I'm so glad you could come." She had an aroma of home-cooked food about her. Doubtlessly she had spent all morning in the kitchen.

And then I saw Mike. He was sitting on the swing surrounded by many of the members of Grandma's family, in his bleached jeans and plaid shirt.

For a moment I felt disoriented and at a loss. What would I say? He was watching me with a penetrating, accusing gaze. Self-consciously, I glanced at Grandma and Iris, wondering if they noticed the silent exchange between Mike and me. Apparently they hadn't; they were cooing noisily over Phillip. I smoothed my brown cotton dress with shaking fingers and slowly walked over to the group by the swing, painfully avoiding meeting Mike's eyes.

Looking around, I saw Mike's father, Bob. The others I recognized from Grandma's careworn photo albums. Everyone seemed to radiate warmth, love, and confidence. I felt envious.

They all seemed to be talking at once. "What a beautiful baby boy; Such a young mother; How do you like your new home?"

I answered the questions perfunctorily, hoping they didn't notice that my smile was forced, my replies less than accurate.

It felt good to be back at Grandma's, around all these wonderful people. The wood-shingled house with its vined porches, the shady oaks, and the old-fashioned flower gardens exuded the same warmth as these people did. Judging from their avidly interested questions, they were as fascinated with my lifestyle as I was with theirs.

During my musing, Mike had gotten up from the swing and was now standing beside me. For one wild moment, I thought he was going to embrace me; but he didn't.

"Where is your husband?" He thrust his hands into the front pockets of his won jeans.

"He is working on his parents' farm." Suddenly I felt awkward. I could find nowhere to put my hands. *Perhaps I should be wearing jeans with pockets,* I thought in half-hearted amusement.

At that moment, Grandma announced from the back porch that the noon meal would be served. Mike and I stood, rooted helplessly in our places in the garden, and watched as everyone made their way into the house.

"We'll be in shortly," Mike called to his grandmother.

She nodded understandingly as she followed the others into the spacious, airy kitchen. Mike's parents glanced knowingly at each other.

Mike watched as everyone disappeared from the back garden, apparently lost in thought.

My hands were shaking worse than ever. I wished Iris would have given Phillip back to me instead of carrying him with her into the house. At least then I would have had something to do with my hands.

Mike looked back at me, his blue eyes cool, "You haven't changed." He paused a moment, "Or perhaps you have. Or perhaps I never knew you at all."

A dead, heavy silence ensued for several moments.

"Why didn't you tell me, Rachel?"

I felt hot with remorse.

"I must say, considering how young and naive you appeared to be, you were very adept at leading me on."

"Oh, Mike, please." I choked on his name. "I wanted to tell you. I never had a chance."

"You would only have needed to contact me through Grandma, or something." His voice rose. "But you couldn't, could you? Ask for my help, that is. You're much too proud. You have to do everything by yourself, don't you?" He ran frustrated fingers through his luscious hair. I gazed at his classical features, now alight with anger. "I'm your friend. I could've helped you. I know this marriage is a farce. You look miserable."

I felt drained by his outburst.

Suddenly his voice became soft, and he smiled as he hugged me close, "I'll never stop caring for you, Rachel."

I smiled in return, and soon we were both laughing.

"You have a beautiful son."

"Thank you," I clasped his hands in gratitude.

"He should be beautiful. Look at you."

"Oh Mike," I loved his flattery.

He lifted my chin, "My little Amish girl, so lovely, so cruel." He paused briefly. "Do you still have the crystal?"

I nodded, and we embraced; then made our way to the house to join everyone in the kitchen.

"Then all will be well," he said.

chapter 16

On December 7, 1976, I gave birth to an absolutely magnificent baby girl. I named her Regina. Alan thought it was a nice name. The birth was an easy one compared to Phillip's birth.

She was perfect. Her dark hair curled over her ears and down to the nape of her neck, and her skin was as soft as an April morning. Instantly, I was in love.

The stay at the hospital was much less frightening that time than it had been with Phillip. I was fascinated with the purity of the nurses' white uniforms and their professional manner. The nurses and my doctor alike made frequent comments about what a young-looking mother I was.

Upon my insistence, Phillip had stayed with my parents during my hospitalization. He greeted me ecstatically when we picked him up on our way home from the hospital. His chubby hands gripped around my neck as he chattered endlessly. By now he was saying almost everything, speaking fluent German. Along with the rest of the family, he admired Regina, touching her reverently and making remarks about her beauty in awed tones.

The first few months after Regina's birth, I was watched more closely by the church than I had ever been. It seemed as though I would soon have to ask the elders permission to breathe. The main source of their aggravation was the way I dressed Regina. Many times after church services they would have a *rotd* (council) in which I was soundly admonished about the evils of the prideful way I dressed my infant daughter, of course referring to the lovely pastel dresses, soft shawls, and colorful blankets—Grandma Shelhorn's afghan being one of them. I was firmly instructed to "destroy those worldly looking pieces of apparel immediately." Of course, I never did and, consequently, I was always in trouble.

Alan was constantly pressured by his parents to "set Rachel straight," and at one point Martha suggested that she could sew clothes for Regina and he could burn the "other" clothes.

Alan neither advocated nor reprimanded my stubbornness, as usual, he was simply passive.

I had nightmares about spending the rest of my life fighting helplessly and ineffectively against a stern, uncompromising system and then dying at an early age of sheer exhaustion and defeat, unfulfilled and disheartened.

chapter 17

The filth in the house was unbelievable. The wallpaper sagged in the corners, and huge cracks raced diagonally across the walls. The windows were gray with dirt, and layers of dust graced every sill and all the woodwork. The yard was overgrown with weeds and occasional clumps of grass. Neither the fact that the entire outside of the house badly needed paint, nor the fact that it had been raining a steady downpour the last two weeks could dampen my spirits. We were finally moving into our own home!

The farm was only a mile from Alan's parents. Trudging through the waist-length wet grass and weeds towards the dilapidated barn with my sister Hannah, I couldn't help remarking, "The house close to Mother and Father was much nicer, wasn't it?"

Hannah glanced at me, "But it was too close to us, wasn't it? That's why Aaron didn't buy it." Her astute observations amazed me. She was only fourteen years old.

"Heil Hitler!" I saluted smartly, and Hannah giggled at my scathing reference to Aaron.

It was just last Saturday that the purchase of our farm became final. It was all very sudden. The previous owners, an aged couple who were barely able to care for themselves, moved to Indianapolis to stay with their daughter, so the farm was sold.

The barn wasn't in any better shape than the house. The loft was sagging dangerously, and I remarked to Hannah that at this point it probably wouldn't be advisable to walk under it.

Dry, dusty hay crunched under our feet as we entered the barn.

"Oh!" Hannah and I both jumped and screamed as a rat scurried from somewhere, under the hay, disturbed by our footsteps and raced to the empty corn crib built on one side of the barn. Looking apprehensively back at the decrepit house, I wondered how many rodents made their home there. Shuddering with chills of disgust, Hannah and I both quickly returned to the waiting carriage.

"I'll help you do all the work, Rachel. Don't you worry for one minute," Hannah assured me sweetly.

God, I love her. I could see more of myself in her everyday, a thought that secretly made me despair. *Would discontent and a hungry spirit well up inside of her and threaten to choke her as it did me? Oh God, give us both strength.*

Mentally, I began going over what we would need to make the house livable. Gallons and gallons of paint for starters, I decided quickly. New floor coverings in the bathroom and downstairs bedroom. Nicely printed linoleum would do.

Alan pulled in Aaron's carriage behind us as we drove into the yard by the tool shed. He alighted and tethered the horse to the hitching post by the shed and came over to our carriage. It was misting fine drops of rain and the whole countryside was foggy and gray. He looked tired and worried; he always looked tired and worried.

"Hannah and I were up inspecting the farm," I called out to him. Ribbon chomped impatiently at the bit, anxious to be unhitched. "There's lots of cleaning and painting to be done in the house."

"Before you start painting, you have about ten acres of corn to get out that wasn't harvested last fall," Aaron's abrupt guttural tones rudely prevented Alan's reply. He had come from behind our carriage from the horse barn where he was apparently doing evening chores.

Smiling brightly at his sour expression, I replied, "So we will shuck the corn in the mud. It's no problem. And besides, I'm sure you'll help us, seeing as how we've helped you so much." I glanced laughingly at Hannah.

"Humph," was Aaron's only answer to my brilliant suggestion.

A short while later, Hannah and I entered the kitchen through the side door from the porch. Regina was content in her swing that I had purchased on one of our trips to

Shelbyville. Phillip was being entertained by Mattie with a picture book I had purchased the same day that I got the swing. Martha, of course, again had thought I was being quite extravagant and had informed Alan that my children would soon be as spoiled as I was.

For the next three weeks we toiled in the cornfield down on our farm. The mist and fog never seemed to lift; it began to seem like a dream world, all gray and silent. I began to wonder whether the farm was really ours, whether it was actually real. The corn and the mud certainly were real, as real as the soreness and aching in every bone and muscle in my body.

A few times we were assisted by Alan's sisters, but for the most part, it was Alan, Hannah, and I who got the corn out of that sopping field that spring.

Mother had generously offered to keep the children for me during the time we were preparing the home for moving in.

It was early morning at the breakfast table at the Warners.' Everyone bowed their heads for a moment of silent prayer. My lack of devotion appalled me; I was not so much thanking God for the food as I was thinking about all the painting that lay ahead of me.

After the meal, I remarked to Alan, "After today the corn should be finished, and then we can go buy paint."

Aaron and Martha exchanged knowing looks.

Late afternoon we finally finished. Hannah and I both shrieked with joy and jumped ecstatically up and down, splattering mud into our boots and onto our skirts. Alan watched us with puzzlement and a touch of envy.

"Now we can go buy the paint and start cleaning up the house," I announced as we rode up from the field on top of the corn wagon bouncing about on the fruits of our labor. As the cumbersome wagon drew closer to the corn cribs, I noticed Aaron standing close to the barn, watching our arrival. He finally decided to show his face, now that the corn was all out of the field.

Hannah and I both ignored him as we shoveled the corn into the crib.

Alan and Aaron conversed at length by the barn walking slowly around the decrepit building, discussing renovation plans.

Hannah and I both sang *Ach du lieber Augustine* all the way home.

I saw them as soon as we pulled up in the yard by the tool shed. Gallons and gallons of paint stacked imposingly under the lean-to roof by the shed.

"Oh by the way," Alan remarked hesitantly as he saw me staring at the paint. "Mother went out and bought paint for our house today. She also got some new floor covering for the bathroom."

I was so choked up with anger I couldn't speak. Hannah watched me with wretched pity. I hate pity.

"How did she know what colors Rachel wanted?" Hannah inquired of Alan.

"Oh, she just got the color she thought would be best."

"But I wanted to get the paint and floor covering," I finally choked out.

Shaking with frustration and freezing anger, I alighted

and stalked off toward the milking barn, Hannah close on my heels.

Martha was pouring milk from a stainless-steel pail into the huge bulk tank cooler when we burst into the milking parlor a few moments later.

"I would like to speak with you," I spoke slowly and distinctly, ice dripping from my voice.

She looked up in feigned surprise.

"What's wrong?" She rearranged her milking skirt about her misshapen body.

"That is my house, and as such I should be able to choose the colors with which to paint the walls. Who is going to live there? You? Or I?"

"Furthermore, it seems to me that you have enough to concern yourself with without worrying about telling me what colors to paint my walls," I smiled coldly.

Martha's face was white with shocked amazement; Hannah looked enormously amused and, with a visible effort, suppressed a giggle. Martha stormed out of the milk house, no doubt to tell on her awful, wayward daughter-in-law.

When we came back up to the yard by the tool shed, Ribbon was still hitched to the carriage, tethered to the hitching rack.

"Let's go back up to our farm," I suggested to Hannah, who immediately advocated my idea. Hurriedly, I untied Ribbon from the post and told Hannah to get into the carriage. As we raced down the driveway, I caught a glimpse of Alan running out across the house lawn waving for us to come back.

Taking the blanket from off the carriage seat, I assured Hannah that we were much better off coming back down here and giving Martha time to cool off. Martha was likely in the house at this moment, giving Alan another account about his insubordinate wife.

Spreading the carriage blanket in one corner of the dingy living room, Hannah and I sat cross-legged on the floor and began discussing the recent events.

For what seemed like hours, I poured my heart out to Hannah.

"Should we go back home tonight?" Hannah finally asked. She meant home to my parents.

"Yes, we should perhaps. I miss the children so much. Do you suppose they still look the same?"

Hannah laughed, "You saw them just two days ago."

We both looked up through the window as another carriage entered the driveway. It was Alan.

"What does he want?" Hannah looked at me inquiringly.

Attempting to ignore the painful knot of apprehension in my throat, I answered airily, "Oh, I'm likely in trouble."

Alan's face was white as he entered the dingy room, "Why did you speak to my mother like that?" His fists were clenched at his sides.

Hannah was watching Alan, mesmerized.

"Your mother had that coming for a long time," I finally answered carefully.

I felt his hot breath on the back of my neck and smelled the rancid odor of his work-stained clothing.

Hannah jumped to her feet, still watching him, "No, don't do that!"

Suddenly, Alan's rough, sweaty hands clenched around my neck and wrenched me to my feet.

Pushing me up against the wall, he began beating my head against the stained, faded wallpaper. I was sick with terror. His eyes were glazed. "No! Stop!" my screams were muffled from the gagging hold he had around my throat. For what seemed like an eternity, he beat my aching head against the wall, at times releasing his grip to slap me stingingly across the face.

Hannah was screaming with horror and fright. By this time I was too exhausted to do anything, much less fight back.

Dazed with pain, I don't remember when Alan left. Hannah looked shocked and bewildered.

"Goodness, we haven't had dinner yet. Are you hungry?" I asked on our way back to Warner's.

"No."

"Hannah, please don't say anything to Mother and Father...please."

"Why?"

"Because you just can't," I spoke through swollen lips, clasping Hannah's hands in mine urgently.

When we entered the kitchen a few moments later, Aaron and Martha looked at me smugly, as though saying, "There now, I guess you were put in your place." The smell of the milk, soup, and eggs they were having for their evening meal nauseated me. Alan's little brothers, sitting in a tight row with their homespun shirts, suspender pants, and messy hair watched me curiously

A few moments later, looking into the mirror above the dresser in our bedroom I remarked to Hannah, "Now I understand why they all stared at me so." My face was a mess, all swollen and bruised, with drops of blood oozing from the welts on my cheeks.

Hannah sat down on the cot in one corner of our bedroom where she slept during her stay here and began sobbing hopelessly.

"Oh, Rachel, it's so unfair. How can you put up with this?"

Sitting down beside her, I clasped her in an apologetic embrace.

"Don't worry, Hannah, everything will be okay. We must be strong. Someday, things will be much better. We can't let this get us down and break our spirits." The truth was I hated the whole lot of them.

Alan never spoke to me when he came up to our bedroom a few hours later.

The next morning, I called Mr. Phillips and asked him to take Hannah and me to Shelbyville where I bought paint in lovely pastel colors to paint my walls. I also bought beautifully printed linoleum for the bathroom and bedroom. Several times I caught curious looks from store clerks inspecting my traumatized face. My father had given me money when the farm was first purchased for the improvements. I never told Alan and kept the money hidden until now.

Mr. Phillips never mentioned it, but I think he knew where the bruises came from. Then we arrived back at the farm with the paint, he grasped my hands urgently and said, "Please take care, okay?"

Hannah opened her mouth as if to say something and then quickly closed it at my warning look.

That evening we went to see the babies at my parents. Alan acted as though the beating had never happened.

Father and Mother both asked me what happened to my face. I told them I fell down the stairs. I don't think Mother believed me; I know Father didn't. He never spoke to Alan that evening and coldly ignored his presence.

Within two weeks, Hannah and I had the house all clean and painted. My mother came over a few days with my other sisters to help also.

Alan came up every day to work on the barns and on several occasions even helped us paint. During this time, he was always kind and courteous. It was hard to imagine he could turn into such an animal. It really was understandable why Martha didn't help clean or paint. Late in April, just a few days before we moved into our own home, she gave birth to a girl, whom she named Fannie Mae. It made me think of the boxes of chocolates Mike used to bring to Grandma Shelhorn's.

Our own home! With Hannah at my side, we went from room to room, inspecting our handiwork—beautiful new curtains in pastel shades I had sewed, clean, freshly painted walls and the beautiful floor covering Alan had so expertly installed.

"Oh, isn't it wonderful!" I embraced Hannah ecstatically.

She smiled lovingly and patted my back, "Oh, Rachel, you deserve it. You must be the bravest person I know."

Phillip was running about from room to room, joyously exploring his new residence. Regina cooed happily from her swing in one corner of the living room, which was now furnished with heirloom furniture that had been given to me from the family stores.

Why shouldn't I be brave? I had so much to be thankful for, so much to look forward to. My children and I had a wonderful future waiting for us. I just knew it. God said that through Him all things were possible, and I knew Him would never let me down. And besides, I still had the crystal. Whenever I looked into its iridescence, I saw hope and love and faith.

chapter 18

Joseph

Joseph was almost content. Rachel and Alan were living on their own farm now. Well, not quite their own. Aaron had purchased it for them after he found it to be to his liking.

Rachel could come to visit her parents now without being indicted by the Warner's. Joseph could have his family together more often.

Emmanuel was too quiet. Joseph saw himself in his eldest son. He could read the dreams in Emmanuel's wistful eyes, recognizing his own hopes of a fleeting yesteryear.

Memories of the few short years he had left the Amish

when he was Emmanuel's age passed clearly before him. Studying at the university in a large midwestern city, awed by the ways of the outside, overwhelmed and intrigued by the wonder of a new life. He could never forget his mother's wailing cries when he came home to visit that weekend in "worldly clothes." The hysterics she displayed were a ploy to convince her son to come back to "the church."

He had to come back. He could never cause his mother such grief.

Now as Joseph watched his wife and daughters piece together a beautifully crafted quilt, he saw the truth in Emmanuel and Rachel's faces.

"Sure is good to have you here for the day, Rachel," Emmanuel patted her shoulder and playfully pulled out a thread she had just painstakingly woven through the fabric.

"What do you think you're doing?" she demanded, then grinned at his wounded look.

Joseph smiled at their camaraderie. *An unspoken communication between those two.* He knew they would never fit the mold of their people, just as he hadn't. There was no tangible evidence of that, just an instinct. Rachel was becoming more like the daughter he once knew, strong and assertive. He was glad, but also wary. He knew those characteristics would lead Rachel to the same actions that he had once initiated. Those that had made his mother weep while his father stood by, grim and disapproving.   Rachel's next comment strengthened his instincts, "I saw some ready-made quilts at Sears last week. Why don't we just buy those instead of making all this work for ourselves?"

Sarah looked up sharply, "Those are worldly things we

must stay away from." She glanced at her husband, seeking approval, "Anyway, 'longsum' is better." For a moment, there was silence as the quilters diligently wove the heavy silk thread through the cotton fabric creating "The Star of Bethlehem" pattern. Presently, there was a tea break, and, shortly thereafter, Emmanuel and Joseph went back out to cultivating the corn.

Joseph was almost content—but not quite. Always there was the lingering doubt, questions of what could have been. Just as Rachel and Emmanuel, he was not quite happy. But he would never say that to anyone. That must forever be his secret. No one could ever know of the conflict that raged relentlessly within him, year after year after year.

Hannah was staying with us again.

It seemed she was behaving rather strangely of late. We frequently engaged in lengthy conversations about our culture and our restlessness concerning it. Hannah revealed to me that she was as dissatisfied with it as I was. Perhaps that explained her odd behavior.

One morning, I lay in bed as long as possible, stretched out lazily under the cool sheets in my cotton nightgown. Sleepily, I wondered to myself where Alan was, already out of bed before the crack of dawn. *Oh well, he must have started the chores earlier today then usual,* I decided as I rolled over and pulled the pillow around my head. Just as I was drifting off to sleep again, I heard a soft movement upstairs, then murmuring voices. *Oh yes,* I thought, *Hannah is sleeping upstairs. Then, I wonder who she is talking with? Alan!* My mind instantly knew the answer. Alan was upstairs with Hannah. How strange. He and Hannah never said anything to one another about anything more than the weather and how well the garden was doing. What was he doing in Hannah's bedroom in the early morning hours? *I should go up and see,* I reasoned and then decided, no, *I'll wait and see what happens.* In a few moments Alan came quietly down the stairs. Rolling over onto my stomach, I pretended to be asleep.

After he left the house, I got up and quickly dressed in my homespun dress. Barefooted, I tiptoed into the children's room and kissed each of their sleeping faces.

After the milking was finished, Alan hitched the two percheron horses up to a cart and left for his parents to help his father cultivate corn.

Hannah and I spent most of the day tilling the garden and mowing the lawn. Many times I tried to summon up the courage to ask Hannah about Alan's early morning visit to her bedroom, but words failed me.

The following Sunday evening after the milking was finished we went to my parents' for dinner. My spirit was growing visibly stronger. Father watched me proudly and commented on the returning bloom in my personality. My friend Esther and her new boyfriend were also guests, along with her parents. After a meal of chicken and noodles and Mother's homemade bread, the men and boys played a game of croquet. Esther held Regina and informed me that she wanted, more than anything, a white house with a big kitchen and six children.

Emmanuel stayed by himself, closing himself off from the activities of the rest of the family, rarely speaking and declining the invitation to croquet.

Presently, he disappeared out the front porch door and began slowly walking down the dirt path that led to the back of the farm to the old barn where he'd always hidden his guitar. He had almost disappeared into the trees and foliage by the time I finally caught up with him.

I grasped his arm urgently as he continued to trudge through the underbrush, hands in pockets, head down. "Oh, Emmanuel, talk to me," I pleaded breathlessly, winded from my run back to the barn.

He continued to ignore me, "Look, Emmanuel, I know there's something terribly bothersome on your mind. We used to talk. Why can't we now?"

"Talk about what? No one ever hears what I'm saying anyway."

"Emmanuel, you know I'll hear you."

By now we had reached the barn and stepping inside, Emmanuel motioned for me to sit down on a stack of old lumber beside him.

His thin, lanky frame was tense as he fidgeted with his suspenders for a moment and nervously scratched his head, his thick dark hair ruffled from his anxious movements.

"Father found my guitar. I had it hidden away up there," he pointed to the stack of hay bales, dusty with age. "He destroyed it. I can't stand it. I had nothing else."

"Oh, Emmanuel!" I sobbed, heedlessly clinging to his

thin frame with futile sympathy. "What are you going to do?"

"I cannot tell you what I'm going to do, for at this moment I really don't know. But I will know soon." His chin stiffened, his shoulders straightened.

We sat on the molding lumber in the ancient barn that late summer evening, discussing at length times gone by. No one mentioned our long absence when we returned to the house. Father watched us both knowingly, he knew that Emmanuel had confided in me. Shortly afterwards, we left for home.

Early the next morning while I was doing laundry in the Maytag wringer washer that Aunt Mary had given to me, Mother and Father arrived with Henry.

They walked urgently up to the enclosed porch. Father's face was stern; Mother's face was ashen with grief.

"What is wrong?" I asked, quickly grabbing Father's hand.

"Emmanuel is gone," Father said.

"Gone?"

"Yes, his bed was made this morning, his closet empty," Mother's voice was trembling. "I think you know about this."

"No, I swear to you, I don't."

"Don't swear, child. It is a sin," Mother reprimanded me sharply.

"Father, I don't know where he is. I didn't know he was going to leave."

"I don't suppose you would tell us even if you did know,

Rachel. You children have always had a way of sticking together, especially you and Emmanuel."

A week later, I received a letter postmarked Nappanee, Indiana.

Dearest Sister,

That night after we talked and after Mother and Father were asleep, I packed my clothes into the old brown suitcase and hitchhiked my way to Indianapolis where I got on a bus and came up here to Nappanee to stay with Uncle Neal. He helped me get a job in the cabinet shop where he works. The Amish up here are much more liberal than any I've ever know. We are allowed to work in factories, and I even have a ten-speed bike.

I just couldn't tell you that evening what my plans were. I knew you would lie for me. I just couldn't put you in that position. I love, respect, and admire you more than anyone I've ever known.

Be happy, my dearest sister, and never lose your hope and faith.

Your love and spirit will make you great.

Love always,
Emmanuel

chapter 19

The terror in the young man's heart was mirrored poignantly in his eyes as he clumsily packed a few articles of clothing into a worn leather suitcase.

He glanced anxiously around the bedroom one last time before tiptoeing down the stairs. The house was silent, asleep. Ever so softly, he opened the door to his parents' bedroom and gazed upon their slumbering faces, drinking in every detail of each caring line and crease and expression, barely discernable in the blue light of very early morning.

"I'm sorry," Emmanuel whispered. "But I cannot be the person you want me to be anymore. I must be able to breathe."

Later, on his way up north, riding one of those "big buses" out of Indianapolis, Emmanuel sighed, and great tears welled up and spilled unheedingly down his thin cheeks.

His thoughts raced. *And Rachel. Oh God. Married to that animal and his animal family. And Mother and Father pretending like everything is okay. I cannot bear it anymore.*

In the weeks and months that followed, however, the wounds began to heal and the guilt became less severe.

After all, Emmanuel was still a member of the Amish church, he reasoned, even though it was much more liberal. And he kept busy with his job, planing and finishing the wood that would be built into beautiful pieces of furniture. To own a kitchen built by Amish craftsman was to be the subject of envy in even the finest of "outside" neighborhoods.

It made Emmanuel proud. Very soon he was able to afford to rent a small house; and immediately thereafter, he began accumulating every musical instrument imaginable. And what's more, he taught himself to play all of them!

chapter 20

Mother looked drained and troubled. She had come over to help me put up the last of the tomatoes. My sisters were in the living room entertaining the children with wooden blocks that Father had carefully carved for them.

"Sit down, Mother," I motioned to one of the ladder-back chairs surrounding the kitchen table and poured her a cup of coffee.

"What's wrong, Mother? Are you missing Emmanuel?" he had been gone for two months.

"Yes. I am," she sighed heavily.

"Oh, Mother, I miss him too; but he's so happy."

"I'm so afraid we'll lose him to the world," her voice

trembled. "It seems like our family is going to pieces. Have you heard about Aunt Leah?"

"Leah? What about her?"

"Yes, Grandmother Wicky wrote me last week. Leah and her family left the church."

"Mother, you're acting as though they died."

"Oh, but spiritually they have died," she replied earnestly.

"Don't they still worship the same God as you do, Mother?"

"Yes, but they must make a sacrifice! How can living a life of luxury possibly be a sacrifice?"

"Mama, Mama," Regina's tiny voice broke up the conversation as she toddled into the kitchen, grasping a block in her chubby fingers.

Laughingly, I scooped her up and kissed her, "Look at this, Mother, your granddaughter is only nine months old, and already she is running everywhere."

Mother smiled indulgently, and Aunt Leah was not mentioned again.

———————

It was early. Still half asleep, I smiled to myself when I remembered that Hannah had been allowed to stay over for the first time in two months.

I heard a slight movement upstairs. I reached over to the pillow beside me, and with a start realized that Alan wasn't there. My body grew rigid. Memories of the suspicions a few months before flashed through my mind.

Not again, I thought in despair. *Please, God, not again.*

I lay frozen to my spot in the warm bed. Perhaps Hannah should have gone home.

Forcing myself to get out of bed, I threw on my cotton dressing gown and silently crept up the stairs. The sounds were less muted once I entered the stairway. I felt sick.

Tentatively, I tapped on the door to Hannah's bedroom. The movement inside stopped immediately, as though the participants inside were suddenly frozen in a photo.

"Hannah," I spoke softly. "Are you up?"

No answer.

For what seemed like an eternity, I stood there. Then the door slowly opened and Alan stood there, hair tousled, cheeks flushed. He was rigid with guilt.

"What are you doing, Alan?" I asked.

"I was just getting Hannah up to help milk. I thought you might want to sleep in this morning."

"How kind of you," I spoke indifferently, bile rising in the back of my throat. I was going to be violently ill.

Quickly, I went back downstairs and heaved up the remnants of last night's supper into the toilet.

"What's wrong, Mamma?" Phillip stood at the bathroom door, embracing his security blanket.

I felt numb with shock, my mind screaming with denial. *No! No! No!* I held him close, weeping hot tears into his rumpled pajamas.

The morning hours passed in a daze. "What were you doing to my sister, Alan?"

"I told you," was always the angry answer.

Hannah's downcast eyes never met mine. She was terrified. I went to the garden, hoping to lose myself among the greenery. I looked at the house I had just finished painting weeks before. The exterior that seemed so personable yesterday, today seemed so cold and distant; the windows, especially the one in Hannah's bedroom, stared at me indifferently.

"Please take Hannah home," I pleaded with Alan after the morning chores were finished. "And take the babies. I need some time to think."

Immediately after they left, I knew what I had to do: go away for a day or two, even a week. *But my children,* I argued with myself.

I went up to the neighbors across the road to ask for the use of their telephone. I abhorred always asking to use their phone.

"Of course, you may use the phone." Alice Carrigan was the epitome of the all-American housewife: feathered hairstyle, kids involved in school activities, den mother for Girl Scouts. *She must be wondering why I look like death warmed over,* I thought.

I looked up Henry's phone number in the phone book hanging from a chain under the wall-mounted telephone. It was cream-colored; to go with the autumn tones the house was decorated in. Lovely home, cool and conventional. My fingers were stiff, dialing Henry's number in slow motion, my body felt heavy and cumbersome.

"Henry, could you please go over to my parents and ask them to keep the children for a few days?...We'll pick them up later...No, nothing's wrong...Thank you so much."

Where would I go? Considering my father's insistence upon my marrying Alan, would he condone my running away from him now? If I went home to my parents, my father would even turn me away.

On impulse, I dialed Iris's number.

"Hello," my pulse quickened with relief at the sound of her voice.

"Iris, this is Rachel."

My voice was quivering with suppressed sobs. "Please. I have a terrible problem. May I stay with you a few days?"

"Oh yes, of course, dear," her response was immediate; her tones both puzzled and concerned.

As coherently as possible, plans were made that Iris would pick me up at the crossroads down from our farm. I would stay there in the woods until she came in case Alan came back.

Alice was watching me surreptitiously, her perplexity ill concealed.

"Thanks, Alice," I walked slowly towards the door.

"Are you all right?"

"I think so," the sobs tore searingly at my throat, imprisoned by my humiliation.

I raced back to the house and threw some clothes into a bag and went up to the crossroads to wait for Iris.

Where are your people who are supposed to be the children of God? I wanted to scream out loud, but the questions only exploded within me. *If you are such godly, serving, loving people, than where are you now? Where are my mother and father—and the church they so fervently serve? Don't you know I need you?*

The summer breeze quietly ruffled through the branches overhead; the tall grass swayed embracingly around my legs. Picking a tiny blade of grass, I inspected it carefully. *Is God in this blade of grass,* I wondered, drunken with anguish. *He says he is everywhere. Where are you, God?* Fervently, I clasped the crystal pendent I had quickly taken from its hiding place in my dresser drawer just before I left the house.

And with breathtaking swiftness and clarity came the thought, washing over me again and again: *"Be still, and know that I am God..."* (Psalms 46:10, KJV)

I sat quietly under the oaks until Iris arrived and felt God's presence within me, and my heart became less troubled.

After the drive on the interstate and then through countless lovely, shaded boulevards, we arrived at the Byron's home. I thought longingly of the happy time when I had visited this same beautiful home, eons ago, when Michael was there.

"Bob is at work," Iris informed me, warmly clasping my shaking hands. "You are to make yourself comfortable. When you are ready to talk, I'll be right here."

She smiled and kissed my forehead.

I followed her into the house, gasping in appreciation at the large sunny kitchen with its dotted Swiss curtains, bright yellow cupboards, and shiny appliances. It was even lovelier than I remembered.

"Your home is so beautiful," I complimented.

"Thank you, dear," Iris embraced me. She drew back and inspected my tear-stained face carefully.

"What happened, Rachel?"

I drew a shuddering breath.

Shaking my head hopelessly, I spoke with dejection, "I don't know where to begin."

"Well, come on let me show you the bedroom you may

use," she motioned graciously, leading the way through the spacious living room and down a short hallway. She threw open a door to the most breathtaking bedroom I had ever seen. It was all white and gave the illusion of fairyland.

"Oh, Iris," I cried in delight.

After carefully inspecting the billowy curtains, bedspread, and ornate French provincial furniture, I asked hesitantly, "Do you mind if I lie down for awhile?"

"Of course not, Rachel," Iris ran her fingers over my hair. "But won't you tell me what happened?"

Shakily, I sketched out the episode with Hannah; and before I knew it, I was pouring my heart out, with Iris's expression becoming more horrified with my account as it progressed.

"What became of Alan's illegitimate child?" she asked incredulously.

"He is staying with Margaret's parents and thinks Aaron and Martha are his parents."

Iris shook her head slowly, her eyes filled with concern and devotion. "Rachel, you don't ever have to go back. God would never ask that of anyone."

I sank down into the downy bed and drifted into a fitful sleep.

The wind whistled by my ears. I was falling, falling, falling. My mouth was open, but I couldn't scream.

"Oh, God," I tried to speak, but the words were slow and labored. "Please, forgive me of all my sins, for I know I'm going to die."

"Rachel, Rachel," someone was shaking me, "wake up, you are having a nightmare."

Sitting up abruptly, I realized it had been a bad dream. My body was trembling convulsively and dripping with perspiration.

Disoriented because of the new surroundings, it took a few moments for me to realize that it was Mike who was shaking me.

"Rachel, poor little girl," he gazed at me with utter compassion and naked love in his eyes.

I was never so glad to see anyone in my entire life. With overwhelming relief I embraced him, starving for the safety offered.

For hours I talked and he listened, never criticizing my incoherent, aimless utterances. I felt emotionally cleansed and at peace.

"I'm back at the university studying accounting. When my mother called today and told me you were here, I cut class and came over immediately. I sat here and watched you sleep for an hour or more," he informed me quietly as he gently stroked my face.

"Thank you, Mike," I replied fervently, gratitude choking me of any further words. Quickly, I reached into the pocket of my dress.

"Michael, look," I held up the crystal pennant and smiled.

He smiled in return and touched my lips with a gentle finger.

The stay at Iris and Bob's was wonderfully restful; by the third evening, I was missing the children terribly.

Mike spent the evenings there and was marvelously kind. He made me feel cherished and warm. One evening he took me to dinner. It was an amazing place, with soft lights and quiet music.

I had never been in such a mellow place. My habit drew many curious stares, and I began to feel decidedly alien. I scarcely knew how to act. I was afraid I would embarrass Mike, but he seemed proud to have me with him. The clothing the women wore left me breathless. *How exciting it must be to wear such vibrant colors,* I thought enviously.

Mike watched me admiring all the fashions. "You would love to dress like that, wouldn't you, Rachel?"

My attention focused back on him. Hungrily, I gazed into his sea green eyes, my fingers itching to run through his thick, ebony hair.

"Rachel," He gently caressed my hands. "You're so lovely just as you are." The fire in his eyes made my knees weak.

Self-consciously, I turned my face away, afraid of what my eyes would reveal, and even more frightened of the pounding of my heart. *What was I doing? I was a godly person, wasn't I? Do children of God feel these things? I had never felt so drawn to anyone in my life.*

Iris met us at the door when we arrived back at the Byron's home. "Alan phoned this evening," she stated simply, her voice expressionless. "He said he would call back."

"Did you tell him where I was?" My voice was tight.

"I told him you were having dinner with a friend."

I wondered silently how he had discovered my whereabouts.

Mike's shoulders sank several inches as he sat down on the front room sofa and dropped his face in his hands. The soft glow of the lamps cast gentle shadows over his wavy hair.

My heart ached unbearably.

Iris and Bob gazed solemnly at me and then at Mike.

"What will you do, Rachel?" Bob finally asked.

"I miss the children so," my voice broke.

Mike looked up at me and then grasped my hands to pull me down beside him. The urgency in his voice tore at my soul.

"Rachel, please, don't go back. You could bring your children here."

I gazed long and solemnly at his face, anxiously drinking in every detail. I longed to turn back time—back to when he played classic melodies on his guitar in Grandma Shelhorn's garden, while I listened avidly to every note. His blue eyes were no longer merry, but dark with anguish.

He held me close with trembling, desperate arms while Iris sobbed for her son's pain, and I couldn't even shed a tear.

"I must go back for my children's sakes and for my parents," my voice was flat and bitter.

"No!" Mike's tone was adamant and uncompromising. "I resigned myself to losing you once. I will not do it again," angry tears glazed his eyes.

I couldn't bear to meet his gaze. He knew my decision was final. Abruptly, he cast me away from him and strode toward the front door. Wordlessly, he went out and slammed it behind him.

"God!" His screams rent the air with piercing velocity. "I hate her!"

Iris ran to the door and watched her son, great sobs wrenching her frame. As the sound of his sports car faded in the distance, she sank down to the floor mat in front of the door that read "Welcome to our home."

"Rachel, you must leave tomorrow and don't ever put my son through this again," Iris said.

Early the next morning, she took me back to my parents' home. The journey was silent and strained. When we arrived, we embraced as I said quietly, "Thank you so much for helping me."

"Rachel, you come to us any time you need us. I'm sorry about what I said last evening. It's just that Michael has always been such a vagabond, and here he is a few months away from his degree and he is taking life seriously and I think his love for you was largely responsible for that," she paused and rubbed her hands over her eyes, heavy from a sleepless night. "At twenty-eight years of age he falls in love with a woman for the first time in his life. The problem is that you seem to be terribly torn between your love for him and devotion to your people. It must be terribly difficult, and it is unfair that you have to make that choice. I will try to understand."

We kissed each other and then I alighted and walked up to the front door of my parents' gracious home with its mat by the front door that read, "Welcome to our home."

———————

Naked relief bathed my parents' faces as I entered the kitchen a few moments later. They made no critical remarks, but only said, "We're so glad you're back. We were very worried,"

No one asked me any questions about my "running away" as we sat around the table and drank spearmint tea.

The children wouldn't leave my side; and I couldn't bear to stop touching them, embracing them repeatedly.

Shortly, Hannah pulled me aside and asked me to go upstairs with her. We went to her bedroom, decorated in soft blue and sat on the bed.

"Please don't hate me, Rachel. I didn't know what was happening."

"I know."

"Aaron came over yesterday."

"Did he now?"

"Yes, he told Father that you were behaving very wickedly, and it's time Father did something to make you behave like an Amish woman should."

"What did Father say?"

Hannah smiled softly, "He told Aaron that you had every reason to leave. He also told him that he doesn't want to hear another word against you out of Aaron's mouth—ever."

Oh, Father! My throat was tight with sobs of gratitude and love.

He believed in me! Even years of indoctrination had not prevented him from standing up for his "rebellious" daughter. Hannah embraced me, and together we wept tears of devotion and good will.

Mike's stricken face haunted me for months later. I saw it everywhere. I heard his voice. I felt his presence and thought of him incessantly. Deep within me was the innate knowledge that he and I were not yet finished.

Hannah's quotes of my father's words stayed with me, and kept my faith alive.

Book Three

Let me be free to think my own thoughts to choose my own way, to be my own person.

- author unknown

chapter 21

Mother hadn't written in weeks. She would be busy with the harvest and baking pumpkin pies. She would have no time to write to her lost daughter.

The pain was unrelenting, but not like the pain had been that had finally made my decision to leave the Amish church.

"I can't do this anymore," I had told Alan in the end. "I can't stand to have your other child living only a few miles down the road." And Hannah. Her haunted eyes tormented me. So great was my compassion for her that I could scarcely bring myself to speak of her anguish.

"Why did you do that to her?" I had confronted Alan.

He had simply stared at the floor and looked completely beaten. "I feel so small," he said softly.

"That you should," I shook my head helplessly. "I will not let you touch me again. You have violated the life of my sister. God tells me I must forgive, but I won't forget."

"For a long time you haven't wanted me to touch you," his voice grew stronger as he lifted his head. "You are always so far away, almost as if your heart is with someone else."

Such perception for such a foolish man.

"That is why I did that to Hannah," he added triumphantly as though that excuse had just that moment occurred to him.

"So what is your reason for what happened with your sister?" I asked coldly.

No reply.

"Everyone knows," I spoke with hopeless humiliation. "I am so ashamed."

Esther, who had married a nice Amish boy from another community, had been visiting in our area a few weeks past. After church services, she had offered me a piece of pie, then sat her plump pregnant frame next to me and hungrily consumed it after I refused it. I abhorred the pity in her gaze. "I made this," she announced with false brightness. "It is peach custard. We are supposed to make two crust pies for church, but sometimes I like to be different."

"Is being different the same as being bad?" I asked vaguely.

"Maybe," She scraped her plate clean. "You were never bad, though. Just different." She watched me surreptitiously.

"You don't have to stay around here if you don't want to. God will understand." She laid a warm hand over mine.

"I must get away from here," I spoke urgently to Alan.

"Please let us go together." He was so beseeching, "I can not bear to put up with my family anymore."

"I suppose you must come also," I had given my reluctant consent. "For you will need to earn some money to care for a home and the children. I have no training for an outside job and will need your help. I am afraid I couldn't make it alone."

Relief had bathed his face. He was willing to take whatever was offered.

With Emmanuel's assistance, we had purchased a small country home in Northern Indiana (200 miles away) with money we had received from the sale of our dairy cows.

"Why are all the cows going away?" The children had been confused and frightened when they saw the herd being loaded on a huge cattle trailer.

"Because after awhile we will be going away, too," my eyes misted with anguish.

"But I want Tootsie to come with us." Tootsie, the kicking cow, was Phillip's favorite, "Will we see Caleb and Joseph anymore?" Phillip's handsome baby face was wreathed in anxiety.

I had dropped to my knees and clasped him and Regina in a desperate embrace. "Oh yes," I spoke hopefully, doubtfully, and wept like a lost child. Regina simply looked puzzled. She was so young, thank God.

"Mama, don't cry," she lisped.

Wrenching my thoughts back to the present, I tried in vain to concentrate on the task at hand. Trimming the tall grass that grew like young wheat beside the white rail fence surrounding our new home was no small undertaking. Fortunately, we were now living only a few miles from Emmanuel, and he frequently came over to help with the yard work on weekends when he was off work from the furniture shop where he was employed.

"Don't you love it?" His face was bathed in pride of accomplishment when he had phoned us with his find a few weeks before our move away from Shelbyville. "I am so glad I found it for you!" He had looked directly at me, completely ignoring Alan. His bitterness toward him equaled my own, but apparently Emmanuel was willing to extend a vague, cold acceptance. "I guess you will be living here, too," he had finally remarked, looking briefly in Alan's direction.

It was truly a lovely country home if one could see past the neglect. An elderly widow lady had lived there and had been unable to keep up with the yard. It was sadly unkempt. Next would come the painting of the fence and house. *Oh, well, I've done this before,* I thought wryly.

As though drawn by a magnet, my thoughts slid back to the Sabbath morning two weeks before our leaving, when Alan, the children, and I had attended Amish church services for the last time. I had dressed the children in their "Sunday" clothes. We spoke only when necessary, and even the children's endless chatter was absent for once. Although the beginning of an enticing new life beckoned, the end of a poignant, intense period was drawing uncomfortably near. The awareness that my family ties would be severed for a long time, perhaps forever, left me feeling lump-in-throat forsaken.

When we arrived at the home where services were being held, Mother had greeted us at the door that morning, taking Regina into her arms with painful reproach in her eyes. The scrutiny we received from the other devout confirmed that everyone knew of our plans.

Father's smile had been stern, his back rigid, and his face pale as he greeted me with a firm handshake. He had scarcely looked at Alan. Innately, I realized that Father understood why I had to leave.

The following week, with Aaron's adamant predictions of impending hellfire and my father's half-hearted verifications there of ringing in our ears, we had packed our possessions onto the rented Ryder truck. There was no offer to help from either family or friends.

"This truck has two seats," Alan had informed me. "You and the children can sit in back, and I will sit up front with the driver."

Phillip had come trailing slowly from the milking barn just as we loaded the last boxes of canned goods.

"Look, Mama." He held up a leather strap with a cow bell attached. "Can I take this?" His blue eyes were luminous with grief. It was Tootsie's bell. My throat was so tight I could scarcely speak, "Yes, my son."

And so, another chapter of my life came to a close. Phillip and Regina gazed long and hard out the side window as we pulled away from our recent home. They strained to catch a last glimpse of the farm as it disappeared over the horizon. "Good-bye," they said in unison.

With a conscious effort, I pulled my thoughts back to the present and concentrated on clearing away the overgrowth from the last stretch of fence. "Tomorrow I will start painting," I spoke out loud.

Alan would be home from work soon. He would be exhausted from another hard day with the construction company he had found employment with the first week of our arrival. He would have to drive me to Aunt Leah's house a few miles away to get Phillip and Regina. She had offered to keep the children for the day so I could finish the clean-up. In due time, he would come tearing up the drive with his latest obsession, an Oldsmobile Cutlass. He had purchased it immediately after the move, and Aunt Leah's husband taught him how to drive it. His face had been aglow with the most uncharacteristic animation and suggested he take us all for a ride.

The children were enthralled. "We can go fast now," Phillip observed.

"Maybe Grandma and Dad Should get one." Regina sat silently in the back seat, wide-eyed with wonder and nodded in agreement.

"Caleb said they can't because God wouldn't like it," Phillip continued in his child-like German.

A separate God? Musingly, I remembered the question of my childhood. We were outsiders now. Perhaps there was no separate God, but only varying degrees of the same God. Perhaps he expected more from some than others.

With breathtaking pangs of love, I recalled Mike's face as he explained the crystal to me eons ago.

"…many facets…like the potential of the human soul… Was the soul part of God instead of a separate entity that he would judge according to how well one abided by the laws?"

"What did you say?" Alan had glanced over questioningly. Without realizing, I had spoken aloud.

"Oh, it's nothing."

He had watched me quizzically, driving more slowly. "Do you love me?" he asked abruptly.

The children were silent.

"No," I said perfunctorily.

A short while later, as I pulled the last of the grass up from the fence row, Alan came home. Subsequently, we went to gather the children. Aunt Leah looked tired. She had been putting up tomatoes. She and her family attended a local Mennonite church and occasionally would invite Alan and me to come with them. We were, however, not regular attendees.

Emmanuel, on the other hand, remained a member of the Amish church and had not progressed beyond owning a ten-speed and living in a house supplied with electricity and numerous musical instruments. (Varying degrees of the same God. Honor thy father and mother and forefathers.)

Phillip greeted me with an enthusiastic, "Mama, let me show you. I planted something." It was ragweed, wilted and sorry looking. Phillip, the farm boy.

"That's wonderful, son." I smiled and gathered Regina and her Amish doll into my arms and kissed them both.

Subsequently, my family and I slowly began to adapt to our new life. The children seemed content, and Alan enjoyed his work; I thought often of Mike and it made me feel warm inside. His presence in my heart became my security blanket. "Someday," I would whisper a promise to his image.

However, even my love for him could not stem the waves of homesickness and despair that would wash over me when I thought of my family.

"What's the matter, Mama?" My children would attempt to console me on the occasions they would find me weeping. Frequently, the children and I would take walks around the countryside gathering brightly colored leaves that had deserted their places on the trees.

In due time the steady October rain reminded the world that winter was surely coming. Winter and Christmas. Christmas without my family.

Eventually, the periods of desolation began to ebb, as did the heat of summers long passed.

But the pain of breaking away never completely dissipated. To this day I am haunted by the loss.

chapter 22

Two days before Christmas.

The children and I were so homesick; we decided that we would go home, regardless of my father's last words to me, "You don't need to come home ever again unless you repent." That same day I called down to my parents' neighbors and asked them to please take a message to my family: we were coming home for Christmas.

A few hours later my sister Marietta returned my call, "Father said to ask you if you remember what he told you when you left, Rachel." She fumbled over the words. Marietta—always the devoted, obedient daughter.

I could only think how wonderful it was to hear from

someone from home. "Oh, Marietta, it's so good to hear from you! How is everyone?"

"We are all fine. We miss you and the children very much."

"Oh, we miss you too. We'll see you in a few days though. Isn't that wonderful?"

She cleared her throat painfully, "But didn't you hear what I said?"

"Oh yes, I heard. But you must understand that Father said that, not because he means it, but because he feels pressured by family and social position to do so."

I don't know if Marietta understood.

"We'll be there," I continued. "I can't wait. We'll have ham and potatoes and cheese and all the other good food Mother makes. We'll sing together just like usual. For one day we'll pretend nothing is different."

My exuberance was affecting her, "It will be so nice—no, more than nice—it will be wonderful."

"Of course, Marietta, until then, I love you. *Auf Viedersehen.*"

Not until after she hung up did it occur to me that it was strange that Father had sent one of the children to remind me of his parting statement.

The children were ecstatic when I informed them of our holiday plans. Alan seemed indifferent. He didn't suffer from the homesickness that the children and I did, at least not outwardly so. We immediately began preparations for our holiday. We still only wore Amish clothing, so that would at least save my parents the shock of seeing us dressed completely different. It would be distasteful enough for them to see us arrive in an automobile.

It was nearly eight o'clock when we arrived on Christmas Eve. The kerosene lamps were all lit, and the house smelled of oranges and home-baked bread. The furniture, the curtains, and the china in the walnut china hutch looked so familiar, yet so different. Goodness, I had forgotten how huge it was. The relief of being back home with my loved ones was so great I wanted to weep. My sisters greeted us at the door, while Mother and Father remained seated in the living room. The whole house glowed soft gold, the rays from the kerosene lamps reflecting off the solid mahogany and walnut furniture. Both the huge kitchen range and the living room stove radiated warmth and the scent of burning embers. The simple, breathtaking beauty of this home and its occupants hit me with a force that I had never experienced previously. So much love, and…sadness.

My mother greeted me with tears in her eyes and as she embraced the children, great sobs tore from her throat.

My father arose from his favorite chair and came over to me to shake my hand solemnly, "I'm glad you came home, Rachel." His face was pale with suppressed emotion.

My heart sang. My voice trembled, and I wanted to embrace him fondly; but again the social inhibitions of this culture into which I had once again entered for a weekend quelled my impulse, "I knew you would be, Father."

Although Christmas that year was full of love and good will, things had changed. Our lives would never be the same again.

Emmanuel wasn't there. I wanted him to come with us, but he couldn't do that. We were now excommunicated Amish church members. My father would be utterly disappointed with Emmanuel if he were to ride with us, aub *gefallen fon Jesu* (the fallen away from Jesus). That would make Emmanuel an accomplice of our wrongdoing, an advocate of our transgression. My father's reasoning was "what would my parents say if they would find out?"

Of course, he rode with me many times at home, even drove my car a few times.

I tried to explain to my father that the Amish up north were so different. Their practices much more relaxed. His only response to that was "that wasn't the way I was taught."

Alan was treated civilly those few days in my parents' home. My father spoke to him, not because he wanted to, perhaps, but because of his instinctive social grace. He could never be openly rude to anyone.

We went to the Warners' on the eve of Christmas day. It had been a great burden for me, but Alan persistently urged me to go. So I went because I didn't want to mar this beautiful time with any contention. The dinner was stiff and formal, as always. There was not the warmth and love in this house as in my parents'—not even the sadness.

As we had been at my parents, we were seated to eat at a separate table from the rest of the family. That was part of the shunning practice; they couldn't eat with us. This practice being based on I Corinthians 5:11 (KJV), "But now I have written unto you not to keep company, if any man that is called a brother be a fornicator, or covetous, or an idolator, or a railer, or a drunkard or an extortioner; with such an one no not to eat."

The exchange of gifts that Christmas was one-sided. My parents gave us homemade cheeses, a beautifully crafted solid walnut chessboard, quilts, a fruit basket, and numerous small toys for the children. We couldn't give gifts in return. Along with the other shunning practices, they couldn't accept gifts from us.

The Warners' house didn't seem as different as my parents' house had. The attitude in the home, or absence of attitude, was the same as before. The cold, polished hardwood floors, the expressionless walls and windows, and high ceilings were as indifferent as ever. The kitchen still smelled of onions, the bathroom of lye soap, and the bedroom of linens washed in Clorox. The dinner was the same as all the other dinners at the Warner's: fried chicken (plus ham, because it was Christmas), mashed potatoes, corn, dressing, and more desserts than I could possibly name.

On the morning of our departure, the children and I went to wish Grandma Shelhorn Merry Christmas. Iris and Bob were there, spending a few days. Leftover Christmas wrapping and holiday clutter were strewn over the furniture and floors.

"Rachel, how nice to see you! And the children!" Iris embraced me lovingly and then stood back as Grandma kissed me on both cheeks.

"Hello, kid, how is everything?" Bob smiled fondly at me and clasped my hands. He turned to the children and invited them to come with him to see the tree in the front room.

"Please sit down," Iris motioned to a kitchen chair. She

poured a cup of coffee and handed it to me. I leaned over and placed an arm over the back of Grandma's chair and watched her as she painstakingly packaged up leftover ham in freezer bags. For a long while we sat around the table and caught up on what was happening in their lives and mine. Iris began clearing the table of breakfast dishes. She glanced surreptitiously at me, took a deep breath and then spoke, "We were all together for Christmas. We had a wonderful time, but we missed Michael."

I clasped my trembling hands together, "He wasn't here?"

"No, he said he was too busy, with work and all."

"Work? Where is he working? Where is he living?"

Iris turned from the sink suds dripping from her elbows.

"Oh, he has his degree now. Didn't you know? He's with an accounting firm in South Bend. I understand that's in the same area you're now living."

"Yes, about twenty miles." *Dear God, why was I feeling this surge of ecstasy? Wasn't I supposed to forget Michael? With burning intensity, I wanted to see him again, just for a short while; but no, I could not. I must not.*

Iris watched with a discerning gaze, the conflicting emotions that raced across my face.

"I speak with him on the phone occasionally," she continued. "He doesn't mention your name, but I feel his choice of job location has something to do with you."

"Iris, I'm married," my voice cracked.

She didn't reply and continued the dishwashing, and Grandma wrapped the last of the ham and said quietly, "Michael is a good boy."

The children returned from the front room with candy canes in their hands and, shortly, we left.

"Please come back soon," Grandma Shelhorn pleaded as she hugged me good-bye.

It had been a wonderful Christmas, after all.

For weeks, Michael was with me. His face haunted my dreams; and every waking hour I would fantasize of running into him in town sometime, at a restaurant or a park, perhaps. I wondered how he liked his work, where he lived, and if he still played classical melodies on his guitar.

Eventually, the torment subsided, but the desolation of thinking about not ever seeing him again never left me.

chapter 23

The following spring, I befriended Marion, a winsome, country neighbor. She was my mentor and largely responsible for my introduction to the "outside." She taught me how to drive, how to speak without a "Dutch" accent, and how to dress like all the other housewives on the outside, regardless of the pain it caused her.

"I liked you so much as an Amish girl," she'd say mournfully as she cut and styled my hair in a chic, shoulder-length page boy.

Alan was furious. "What on earth do you think you're doing?" he demanded. "And without my permission!" He would shrug and add hopefully, "Oh well, so long as you don't start wearing pants."

That summer after earning my GED, Marion took me to a local university where I took a college entrance exam.

While I was taking the exam, Marion had taken Phillip, Regina, and Nikki to the zoo. When I met them on the steps of the front entrance to the university later, the children came walking from Marion's car with three puppies tagging along behind. "Where did you find them?"

Marion got out of the car, smiling, and ecstatically cried, "Aren't they beautiful? We found them on the back street by the zoo, and I just couldn't leave them!"

Lovable, impulsive Marion. She loved befriending homeless puppies and confused Amish girls. On the way home we discussed the test, college, and what to do with three mongrel pups. She kept two of them, and Phillip took one. He had already fallen in love with the ugliest one of the three. We called our puppy "Amo" because he was now an Amish dog!

By August, I was informed of an acceptance into three different nursing schools in the area.

Alan's reaction to my new plans was one of tolerance, an attitude of, "My, but what will she think of next?"

The last month of summer was filled with a flurry of preparation for my entrance into nursing school. Phillip would be entering kindergarten, and Regina would be staying at a nursery school while I attended classes. The children were as excited about these new developments in our lives as I was. Alan didn't comment much about anything. Even though I recognized that I probably wouldn't receive much emotional support from him in my venture, the fact that he would be providing a lot of the financial support was enough to summon my utmost gratitude.

I could scarcely believe my good fortune at finally being able to realize a dream: Going to college. Nothing could dampen my spirits.

In my busy schedule of caring for the children, the house and the yard, and harvesting vegetables from the garden, I now had to find the time to register for classes, go to a conference with the dean of nursing, Mrs. Parks, and buy textbooks.

The meeting with Mrs. Parks in the luxurious office was intimidating. I was wearing a new dress, and my hair was immaculately combed back into a neat bun. I wore a crisp white prayer covering. I was still wearing conservative clothes, the only diversion from the Amish habit being that now I wore bright colors and tailored dresses. Slipping a hand into my dress pocket, I clasped with trembling fingers, the crystal pendant. As I surveyed the ornate desk and plush carpeting, I wondered if I had undertaken too much.

Dean Parks surveyed me with a mixture of curiosity and amusement. She was a tall, stately woman, white haired with a surprisingly feminine voice. Majestically, she was seated in her chair, with the expanse of the huge desk separating us. Slowly, she swiveled back and forth, fingers together under her chin, smiling and probably thinking "Well, well, what have we here!"

"Rachel," she spoke my name slowly, distinctly, and with relish. "Shall we begin?"

For the next hour we discussed schedules, demanding

studies, and the grueling routines of nursing school. Dean Parks was clearly fascinated with my background, and at frequent intervals interrupted her lecture on school policy to ask questions about my upbringing.

I left her office, head buzzing with school rules and discipline, wondering what in Heaven's name I had gotten myself into. I felt alone and afraid. For one hysterical moment I wanted to just forget the whole thing. *This whole idea is plain crazy. I'll never be able to do it.* I wanted to share my emotions with my family and couldn't. Then I remembered my father's words spoken so long ago: "You can do what you really want if you want to do it badly enough."

I was sitting in the Introduction to Nursing class not concentrating on the lecture at all. So much had happened. Contemplating on the recent months, I could scarcely believe how much change had come into my life in such a short time.

Phillip loved school, he learned everything so quickly. His teacher, Mrs. Lund, was giving him books to read on the second-grade level. "Phillip is extremely bright," she would often tell me. "Of course he is," I would say proudly.

Regina's love for nursery school paralleled Phillip's love for kindergarten; but as much as they were enjoying their lives, I still experienced moments of paralyzing guilt about my absence from them. School demanded so much time and effort from me. I was taking twenty credits the first semester.

The prerequisite chemistry class I took was quite a struggle, but after that, the classes were fairly easy. I tried desperately to develop what all the professors called "good study habits," but found that with all my other responsibilities, there was not much time left for studying.

This will never do, I brought myself abruptly out of my musing and tried to concentrate on the teacher's words.

"Are you ready to go?"

I looked up from the desk where I sat watching the students clamor over each other in their mad attempt to get out of the auditorium. It was Jean Ellis, a fellow nursing student who I car-pooled with. She lived in Elkhart with her parents. Sharp spoken, pale, and painfully thin, Jean loved to wear trendy clothes.

"I must say, Rachel, you are a space cadet, always daydreaming, always with your head in the clouds."

I smiled weakly and followed her out of the auditorium.

"How do you think you did on the psyche test today, Rachel?"

"Very well. It was easy."

"If you say that one more time, I'm going to scream," Jean said in exasperation. "Everything is easy for you. Just for once I'd like to see you really sweat."

I shrugged. Little did Jean know how much of my life I had spent "sweating."

I was still treated with a certain wariness by the rest of the students; and whenever I entered the cafeteria, a hush would fall as though they didn't know what they could or couldn't say around me.

A computer technology student, John, told me once after he had gotten to know me better, "You know, Rachel, you're really just a regular person, aren't you? It's the clothes you wear that make you seem odd."

I only smiled and said, "I don't mind being odd." John nodded abstractly. He then asked me if I cared to go out to his car and smoke a joint with him, which I declined. I didn't even know what a joint was. At my questioning look he tried to explain. "You know grass…pot." And then I knew even less what he meant.

In due time the first semester passed, and I found myself wondering where the time had gone.

We had once again spent Christmas with my family. The tensions of the year before had mellowed, and instead of the reserved welcome we had received the Christmas before; we were greeted heartily by everyone, including my father. Surely, we were beginning to be accepted.

After a too-short winter vacation, classes resumed at the college; once again I was immersed in studies.

The air was unexpectedly warm for February; one of those balmy days that makes its freak appearance in the midst of frost and cold. My thoughts strayed unrestrainedly back to that first spring on our farm by Shelbyville. Desperate with the responsibilities that were now mine, I would think longingly of times when I had nothing more complex to plan than a garden.

Trudging slowly down the concrete walkway toward the science building, I imagined newly seeded ground where there were only dirty patches of snow on the gray campus lawn. I imagined Grandma Shelhorn's garden so green and lush, where Michael and I met. I squeezed my eyes shut and cast my face skyward, "Michael, how are you doing? Where are you, Michael?"

"Who's Michael?"

Abruptly, I was brought from my musing to see Dr. Hartfeld walking beside me. He was the English 103 Professor.

His face was so young, so unscathed. His writing class was my favorite. Despite the youth in his eyes, there was just the slightest bit of cynicism, as though he had been disillusioned by something or someone. With his green army jacket, hair almost too long, and a worn briefcase, he reminded me of the Michael I had met in the garden long ago.

Shrugging self-consciously, I smiled half-heartedly.

"I didn't realize I spoke aloud."

He watched me curiously. I stared down at my new Nikes scuffing the pavement as I walked. My Amish habit was long gone, and in its place were Calvin Kleins and a preppie quilted jacket.

"Michael is my friend."

"Friend, huh?" Dr. Hartfeld glanced at my blue jeans. "You looked different when you first came here."

"Yes, I know."

"You know, Miss Rachel," he continued with affected humor, "you are some rebel, judging from some of the writings you've submitted. You're a helluva writer, you know," he paused and shifted his bulging briefcase with no handle to his other armpit.

"I was a rebel too, once. The establishment of my era called us flower children." He glanced at his watch. "We have ten minutes till classes. Would you like to tell me about Michael?"

So we sat on a bench beside the walkway, and to this professor I scarcely knew, I confided my agony about Mike.

"You've known him a long time, and yet you carry him with you. Perhaps it is love with you two," he smiled and spoke with dry humor. He stood and held out his hand, "Come, let's see if one rebel can teach another how to write."

chapter 24

The gulf between Alan and I had grown frightfully large. He became progressively more threatened by my rapidly emerging independence. He would come home in the evenings with a dark, stormy expression on his face, apprehensive about "what craziness Rachel has been up to today."

Marion was adapting to my changes no better than Alan was. Her attitude was one of regret and self-reproach that she had facilitated my introduction to the ways of the world. She hated to see me change, as she described it, "from a simple country girl to a college co-ed."

My children were still, without question, the stabilizing force in my life. In the evenings, I would read to them from the now tattered pages of the Living Bible Grandma Shelhorn had given me. I trusted they would be free through God, not in bondage to Him.

"Mama," Regina lisped softly after one such session, "is it okay for me to go to dance lessons?"

"Of course, dear," I kissed her forehead. "You enjoy it, don't you?"

"Daddy says it's wrong," Phillip added.

Caressing Phillip's cheeks, I searched for the right words, "God gave us talents to use. He wants to see us doing what we are best at." The following week, to Alan's chagrin, I enrolled her in an evening ballet class.

I prayed that my children would see the ugliness in prejudice and human judgment.

In contrast to February, April of 1979 came damply. It didn't seem like the ageless, mythical springtime of my childhood. Where had they gone?

My head was throbbing from the efforts I had applied to the biology exam of the last hour. God—I needed a rest!

Then I saw him! On the oval steps surrounding the huge library. I would know his walk anywhere. With the easy grace of a lynx, the man strode up the steps, two at a time.

Uncaring of the water that splashed up from the puddles on the walkway, I raced in wild abandon toward the figure, now approaching the library doors.

"Michael!" I shrieked breathlessly. "Wait, please, I want to see you! Is it really you?"

Reaching the top of the stairs, the man turned and stood still in a posture of numb expectancy.

"Rachel?" His face was pale with shocked disbelief.

Slowing my madcap dash down to a walk, I hesitantly mounted the steps, afraid I might be dreaming. This wasn't really Michael, was it?

The man held out a hand, visible tremors making his grasp of my hand weak.

"Oh, Rachel," his voice was now flooded with glad relief. "It is you!"

"Michael," his name kept passing soundlessly through my lips. I couldn't stop touching him, his face and his hands. I couldn't stop looking at him, devouring every detail with savage hunger. Gone were the tattered jeans, the plaid shirt. The man standing before me was ever so sharply attired in fashionably pleated slacks and an Izod shirt. The dark curly hair that had once brushed his shoulders was now closely cropped around his ears. The once airy gleam in his incredible blue eyes had become a more responsible, sedate glow.

"What happened to you?" I asked. I gasped and returned his wild embrace.

He gazed at me with the same fire in his blue eyes that had so captivated me long ago and then laughingly returned my question.

"What happened to you, my little Amish girl?"

"You first," I stuck a finger at him. My knees were weak from the adrenalin that had surged through my veins.

At Mike's suggestion, we seated ourselves on the concrete banister on the side of the library steps. He studied his dangling legs and then took an awkward, quivering breath, "You know, Rachel, I shouldn't be so overwhelmingly glad to see you." He watched me intently.

Wrapping my arms around my wet legs, drenched from the

puddles I had raced through, I sat lengthwise, facing his profile. "Please, Michael," my voice was soft with urgency. "Let's just not worry about that right now. Tell me what you've been doing? What's with the Izod and Guccis?"

He smiled questioningly at the Calvin's that clung damply to my legs all the way down to my soaked Nikes. He grasped my hand and gently kissed my upturned wrist. For endless moments, we stared at each other.

Letting go of my hand, he shrugged and grinned wicked, "Well, I got tired of fighting the establishment, so I joined it." He paused for a moment, then on a more serious note, continued, "After graduating, I went to work for an accounting firm in Lansing, Michigan, and a few months back I was transferred to South Bend where I took a position as a junior partner in a subsidiary firm of my previous employer."

"Michael, I am so happy for you, and even happier for myself that I happened to run into you," my voice was husky, cracking with emotion.

"So tell me about yourself, little one," Mike reached over and put a hand on my knee. "What have you been doing? And wearing blue jeans! Tsk, tsk!" He rolled his eyes in mock horror.

I took a deep, trembling breath, trying to collect my thoughts. "Well, it's a long story. Are you sure you want to hear all of it?"

And so, on that wet April afternoon, by the library, I filled him in on the dramatic turn my life had taken, the joy, the pain, the challenges, the guilt, the fear.

"Michael, through all this, I never stopped loving you."

"Hush, child," his tones were suddenly abrupt.

After a moment of silence, he took out a business card and wrote a phone number on it. "That is my home and office number. Please call me whenever you can," he entreated.

"I won't ask for your number," he continued. "For I know I would call you, and I don't want to cause you any problems."

I chewed on a few strands of hair that had escaped from the ponytail I wore and tentatively took the card from him. "Thank you," I smiled softly.

Suddenly, I became aware that the flow of students on campus had filtered down to a trickle. The only sounds were that of a distant train whistle and the gentle drip of rainwater from the roof on the library onto the concrete below. The sun tried to break through the cloud of mist.

I began sobbing quietly, great tears welling up and cascading down my cheeks.

"Rachel," Michael held me and rocked gently back and forth. "Please, don't."

"I don't want to go home."

"I don't want you to go either, now that I have finally found you, but you must—for now at least."

I hiccupped convulsively. "The children are probably wondering why I'm late."

"Let's go. I'll walk you to your car," Michael jumped up off the banister and pulled at my hand.

"Okay," I smiled weakly. "Let's take a short cut through the English building."

Michael seemed strangely hesitant but didn't protest.

As we passed by Dr. Hartfeld's open office door, I

pulled Michael back. "Please wait, I want you to meet Dr. Hartfeld."

Tentatively, I tapped on the door that stood slightly ajar.

Michael's sudden shyness became even more pronounced.

"What's wrong?" I questioned in a whisper that echoed off the tiled corridor floors.

"Yes?" Dr. Hartfeld's weary countenance was indication of another grueling day trying to teach "rebels how to write."

As though a curtain was lifted, the weariness on his face dissipated, "Mike, old man, how in the hell are you?"

My mouth dropped in complete amazement as Mike and Dr. Hartfeld embraced like long-lost brothers.

"We were fellow war protestors," Michael explained. "When Tom told me about a Rachel on campus who confided in him about some Michael, I nearly went crazy. I just had to find out if it was really you."

Wordlessly, I pointed first at Dr. Hartfeld then at Michael. Forcing my lips to function, I finally uttered, "You two know each other?"

Dr. Hartfeld smiled broadly and slapped Mike's shoulder.

"We go way back, don't we, old man?"

Mike nodded and scuffed his Gucci's on the tiled corridor floor.

"Way back," Dr. Hartfeld continued. "A couple of hipsters we were, incapable of thinking two consecutive serious thoughts."

Mike laughed suddenly as apparently the memory of some

escapade in the past crossed his mind, "Do you remember the protest in San Francisco?"

Hartfeld laughed triumphantly, "Do I remember? Hell, somebody had to save the cable cars?"

For a long while the two friends indulged in an avid, heated discussion of their obviously frantic participation in the love and peace "hipster" movement, while I stood silently by. Drinking in every minute expression on Mike's animated face, I felt strangely alienated. I knew nothing of the era they were so passionately speaking of. Those were the years when my biggest challenges were moonlight chess games with my father and nude swimming in the river on a secluded Amish homestead. I hadn't even known of the war that was raging out of control and with no direction on the other side of the globe.

"Hello," Mike's soft touch under my chin broke my reminiscence. "Are you still with us?"

"See you tomorrow in English 102," Hartfeld tossed over his shoulder as he hunched over his desk, once more back to work on grading "some of this ghastly crap that some of these rebels turn in."

Then we reached my car, Michael embraced and reverently kissed my lips, my eyes, my neck.

"Ah," his eyes were closed; his face was smooth with relief. "So good to be with you again. I dreamed of this countless times."

"Yes."

"I was so grateful to Tom for just filling me in on your activities and well-being." He spoke ruefully, almost apologetically, "Sorry if it appeared that I was spying on you."

"Oh, Michael," I sighed and clung to him with shameless abandon. "I only wish you'd have come by sooner."

Opening the car door and before I could change my mind, I slid into the driver's seat, "I have to go."

Mike nodded as he closed the door for me. As I rolled down the window, he leaned into the opening and questioned quietly, "When can I see you, Rachel?" His voice was beseeching and persistent.

"Soon," I smiled. "Soon."

As I drove away, I looked in the rear-view mirror to see Michael standing alone on that empty concrete desert with orange parking lines all over it. The sun had finally won its battle over the mist and with violent intensity bathed him in yellow light.

My heart sang, "Soon, Michael, soon."

chapter 25

Joseph

Joseph was relieved to hear that Rachel's wild energy was being channeled into something as productive as nursing school.

He had received a letter from a Michael Byron a few weeks before. The writer informed him that he knew where Joseph's daughter was, that a professor-friend named Tom Hartfeld had told him of a Rachel in his class that had confided in him about an unrequited love for an accountant named Mike.

Mike went on to explain that he would go find Rachel because he loved her first and last and that he expected no meddling from her family. However affronted Joseph felt about the abrupt pseudo-warning in the letter, he admitted to a deep admiration for the unknown suitor.

Somehow, though, the letter did not produce a great deal of astonishment in Joseph. He had sensed there was another love in his daughter's heart even as she married Alan.

Joseph raised his eyes heavenward. "God bless and protect my Rachel," he prayed quietly. With that, he burned the letter in the stack of twigs he had accumulated the day before cleaning a fence row. "God bless you too, Michael," he said.

"What are you thinking, Mamma?" a soft touch brought me out of my reverie.

I looked up from the bed, where I lay contemplating about how much I'd like to see Michael, into the dark blue eyes of my daughter's devastatingly perfect oval face. She was only four years old and already classic lines of sheer beauty were beginning to make themselves known in her cheek bones and in the planes of her forehead. For a moment, I felt breathless with responsibility and love. She plopped herself down beside me without ceremony and further ado, her golden curls bouncing about her shoulder and around her face. I reached out gentle fingers and brushed the hair from her face.

"I'm thinking about everything that happened to us these last few years and about me going to school," I said.

Regina's face took on a thoughtful expression, mature beyond her years. "Phillip said now that we're no longer Amish, we can go more places and do more things." It had been nearly two years since we left; she had only been a baby back then.

"Do you remember when we lived down south and rode in a carriage?"

She hesitated for a moment, "Yes, I remember." I don't know if she remembered or whether she said that because she thought in some way it would please me.

At that moment Phillip came up the stairs, his handsome boy frame covered with dust, cobwebs laced over his silky hair. Grasped in his hands was a tiny rabbit—a baby, no doubt. There was a look of pure joy on his face, "Momma, look. I found it in the woods and chased it into the barn, and it ran into the corner where the old hay is but I dug him out." He paused for breath and beamed at me, "I think he's a baby, Momma!"

For that afternoon, I forgot about the exam I should be studying for and helped my son construct a rickety rabbit pen from some dusty, decrepit boards we found in the barn. Regina was the interested critic of our progress, and I assured her that we would surely have never gotten the task accomplished without her valued advice.

As the sun sunk into the tree line in the distance, Phillip, Regina, and I stood back to survey the rabbit pen we had created, with the tiny rabbit sniffing about inside. Phillip, assisted by Regina, had fed the bunny with a medicine dropper.

When I saw the rapture on my children's faces, I remembered a tree seedling I had planted in the yard of our new home in Southern Indiana, eons ago. It had somehow been my ticket to belonging. Now my children had created this "miracle" out of old boards found in our barn on our new farm. This was their home. They both believed that. And because of the seedling that had taken root and flourished, I knew what my children were feeling.

———————

Shrill and insistent, the ringing of the phone brought me to a reluctant consciousness. Easter break at college was just beginning, and that morning I had allowed myself the luxury of sleeping in.

My head was still numb with sleep as I reached for the receiver. For a moment I considered just letting it ring, disgusted with the rude awakening its harsh tones caused.

"Hello," I murmured sleepily.

"Rachel, hello, how are you?"

Immediately, I was wide awake and the grogginess quickly dissipated.

"Hannah! I'm fine. Oh, I'm so glad you called!" At the sound of my sister's voice, the homesickness that I had almost successfully pushed aside rushed back in fiery, consuming waves. "How is everyone at home? Where are you calling from?"

Hannah laughed, her voice sounding so much more mature that when I'd last been with her. "Not so fast! We're all fine, and I'm calling from Henry's house." Ah yes! Henry. I'd nearly forgotten the man with various, mysterious illnesses.

"Hannah, I wish so much you could visit us soon. You haven't even seen our beautiful home."

"Oh I wish I could," Hannah said longingly, and then added, "but you know how it is."

I knew only too well.

"We were wondering if you were planning on coming down anytime over Easter," Hannah's voice took on a hopeful note.

"Really? Mother and Father want us to come?" My heart nearly burst with gladness, relief pulsed through me like quicksilver. They were beginning to accept us. My voice was thick with gratitude as I replied, "Yes, we've been talking about just that." A lie, of course, Alan and I hadn't been talking about much of anything for weeks, we scarcely saw one another.

"Oh good!" Hannah's enthusiasm was electric.

For long moments we discussed events and people back home. We could scarcely talk fast enough.

In due time our passionate, noisy conversation awakened the children. They padded sleepily into the bedroom demanding their rightful time on the phone with their beloved aunt.

Upon my family's suggestion, the children ended up staying their spring vacation at "Joseph und Caleb, Mum und Dat."

Their joy was complete. With the loving acceptance and innocence of children, they agreed with no reservations to dress "Amish" while they were with my family. It mattered nothing to me what they wore. Their radiant little faces shone with expectation and excitement. A week at Mum and Dats! Paradise!

Their happiness made my day and, indeed, for many days ahead.

The house echoed with restless silence without the

children. I missed them incredibly and tried to remember when I had last been separated from them for any length of time. It had been that time we'd painted and cleaned the house on the farm down south.

To take the edge off the void the children left, I threw myself heartily into every household chore I could possibly think of. When the house was cleaned to a spotless shine, I raked the entire acre and half of lawn.

By midweek, I was bored to tears and about to pull my hair out. God! I couldn't even call my children. It was ironic that I had become so dependent on a telephone, considering that I had lived most of my life without one.

Of course, the telephone. Why hadn't I thought of it before? Dusk was fast approaching, and Alan had informed me earlier of an out-of-town ball game he was going to attend with some friends. The thought of spending a night alone, in this secluded home in the country, was not at all appealing.

Before the impulse left and courage forsook me, I picked up the phone and hastily fumbled through my purse for Michael's number.

"Hello," his voice sounded so close.

"Hi, Michael?"

"Rachel! I didn't think you'd ever call!" Guilt flashed through me. I shouldn't feel such colossal emotion at the mere sound of his voice.

"Yes, well, how are you?"

"I'm taking a few days off work," Michael answered with relish, "and enjoying every moment."

In a short time we were talking just like we had in the old days, as though there was some bond of understanding between us that extended over several lifetimes. I found myself confiding in him my loneliness with the children gone.

All the ecstasy I had felt that day when he "happened" to run into me on campus came flooding back, and all I wanted was to see him again, to be with him.

"May I see you?" he asked.

"Yes."

That afternoon we met in a park in South Bend. We walked for hours, holding hands, talking, and admiring the virgin buds on the bushes and trees.

Presently, we went to a dimly lit, expensive restaurant nestled beside a river. Poignant, melancholy music was playing somewhere.

After the waiter with the white cloth over his arm left our table, wine order in hand, I hummed softly to the music.

"You like Mozart?" Mike kissed my fingers.

"Who?"

"Mozart."

"Who is he?"

"The composer. The one who wrote this music," Mike gestured vaguely.

"Yes, very much, thank you."

"He was a driven man, you know. Vulgar. He was nearly always drunk."

The waiter returned with the wine. *Chardonnay Sauvignon.*

Mike held up his crystal goblet.

"Cheers," he said.

I held mine up also. "Cheers."

"Anyway," he continued, "perhaps I should do that, when I simply cannot tolerate life without you."

"Do what?" I asked.

"Buy some vineyard in California and drown myself in the cup, like Mozart did." He laughed humorlessly.

"He did?" I was mortified. "What a misfortune—and being so talented."

"Yes," Mike stared into the swirling depths of the wine goblet. "But there is no pain in oblivion, do you suppose?"

I shrugged.

"Some say it was not his genius, but his love for a woman that drove him to his deadly habit." Mike spoke softly and distinctly, carefully watching my face. He looked terribly morose in the flickering candlelight.

We finished our meal in silence after which I thanked him graciously, and we parted to go to our respective homes.

chapter 26

The children talked for weeks about the wonderful time they'd had at my parents during Easter vacation. They loved the singing, playing with Joseph and Caleb, and especially hunting Easter eggs.

It is ironic that the Amish don't believe in having Christmas trees, considering that a heathen practice; but, interestingly enough, they do color and hide Easter eggs.

I envied the delight of the children. It saddened me that they were allowed an amicable relationship with my family and I was not. The anger in me, I had convinced myself, had long subsided and only the hurt remained.

The hungry, volatile thoughts I had harbored that night

in South Bend with Michael constantly haunted me. Had I sinned? Had I transgressed against Alan with my unfaithful intentions?

Alan was gone so much those spring days. My going to school was obviously taking its toll on our already fragile marriage. There were times when he was away half the night and I found I really didn't care.

Because he was so threatened by my somewhat erratic, but rapidly emerging identity, he constantly challenged me and attempted to prove his power over me. He accused me of ignoring him and simply going my own way. Perhaps I did.

Often, I longed to make Alan understand how hard I was working to make something of myself and realize some of my goals, goals I had cherished since childhood. Because I realized where he was, how he was taught, and how he believed, the sympathy of old was always there, even though I defied him.

Our arguments were endless and fruitless. As much as I hated his constant interrogations, he hated when I informed him of being too indoctrinated, "Don't use those big words. I don't even know what they mean,"

The last few weeks of spring semester our nursing class was scheduled for clinical training in the state psychiatric hospital in Lansing, Michigan.

Because of dorm accommodations provided by the hospital, the students would go up and stay from Sunday evening until Wednesday. The children would stay with "Aunt" Carol during those times. She was a middle-aged widow neighbor who came by the summer before to admire my flowers and had immediately thereafter adopted the children and me as her own. She reminded me of a younger Grandma Shelhorn.

My thoughts strayed unrestrainedly to Michael. *Perhaps I can see him again,* I thought eagerly and then immediately reprimanded myself.

It was a warm, late April day. We had just picked up the children at a neighborhood Sunday school.

After the noon meal, I began to pack for our first three days at clinic.

"Are you going to the hospital school today?" Phillip's sad voice made me wince. Pangs of guilt (always the guilt!) raced through me.

The children were helping me pack. I hated to leave them, feeling like the negligent mother I was nonverbally accused of by the women at church.

Regina watched me with her dark, blue eyes opened wide, waiting for me to answer Phillip's question. "Do you have to, Mommy?" she asked in trembling tones.

I knelt between them on the floor and clasped an arm around each of them, searching for words. "Yes, I have to go. But it won't be long any more, then I can stay home in the evenings again. Sometimes we have to do things we don't want to do, so we can get what we're working for," I wondered if they understood.

Alan came to the bedroom door, restless and irritated about my leaving again. I'm not sure whether he was unhappy about seeing me go, or about having the full responsibility of the house for a few days. At any rate, he was clearly in a volatile mood. His eyes caught sight of the jeans I was placing in the baggage. "What are you taking that for?" he demanded.

"I need other clothes to change into after duty."

"But do you have to take those tight pants? They're disgusting."

"But I like them; they're comfortable."

"You look like a hussy in them."

His fury was mounting, and I was becoming increasingly more nervous. Glancing apprehensively at the children whose gazes were now distressed and anxious, I entreated Alan, "Please, let's not frighten the children. You don't like to see me in these jeans simply because you are not used to seeing me in them."

The expression on his face clearly indicated that he thought my defense was a bunch of poppycock. He propped himself defiantly against the doorpost, with an uncompromising expression on his face. "You are not leaving this house unless you leave those jeans at home."

"Oh, come on, be reasonable." I was trembling with indignation and anger, but hesitated to be too argumentative, fearful of what his retaliation would be. But greater than my fear, was hatred for the feeling that his telling me what to do gave me. I simply abhorred having my freedom compromised. Goodness, hadn't we left our family and an entire society to escape just that?

With shaking hands I placed the jeans into the suitcase. Alan lunged toward me from the doorpost and tore the jeans from the suitcase and threw them forcefully onto the floor. "You're seeing someone after school hours, aren't you? That's why you're taking these jeans. Well, we'll see about that. I'm going to burn them."

"No!" I gasped. "You can't. They're Calvin's. They're too expensive to burn!"

"You should have never bought them."

By this time my fury matched his.

Defiantly, I picked the jeans up from the floor and put them back into the suitcase. The children were cowering fearfully on the far side of the bed.

Crack! My head spun, dizzy with pain and surprise. "Oh no, please, don't hit me!" I begged Alan to stop, seeing his hand raised to once again hit me. Flashbacks of that horrible evening on the farm down south nearly drove me to hallucinations.

Repeatedly he banged my head against the bedroom doorpost until my ears rang with pain. Longingly, I looked at the telephone. Intercepting my glance at a possible source of aid, he quickly went to the phone and disconnected the jack from its socket.

Aching with exhaustion and pain, I sank down on the bed. Great sobs of helplessness and fear tore from my throat and shook my tired body.

"Don't hit Mommy," Phillip screamed at Alan, his voice shrill with fright.

Dead silence filled the room and stretched out for an eternity of seconds. I looked up to see Alan standing, head down in shame, face flaccid with humiliation and self-disgust. Sitting down on the bed beside me, shoulders bent, head in hands, he spoke in muffled, broken tones, "I'm so sorry. This change in our lives is so great. I don't know how to deal with it."

Something snapped within me and shook the very core of my being. I went to my children. Speaking in a voice so cold and distant it felt as though someone else were speaking.

"Get out," I spoke through clinched teeth to Alan's bowed head. "So help me God, you will never, ever hit me or belittle me, or control me again. All these years I have struggled to survive and maintain a shred of self-respect. Before I married you, I tried to acquire esteem by attempting to gain the approval of my father, my family, and my people and failed miserably, at that! Then I thought that if I were a good wife and mother and stood by you as best I could, then people would love me. And never once did I gain self-respect from any of this."

Alan had lifted his head and was watching me with open-mouthed wonder.

I stood up from my position on the floor still holding the children close to my side. "Now get out," I repeated.

Alan stood motionless, obviously not being able to believe his ears. When he saw the controlled, tight-lipped anger that etched my face, he slowly inched his way out of the bedroom and out to the front door. He stood for a moment with his hand on the latch, completely bewildered.

"I will have your things packed and sitting on the porch. You may come by and pick them up tomorrow."

"Where will I go?" he finally mentioned pitifully.

"That is not my problem." *God! This felt so good!*

I did not make it to class the next day. The children and I packed their father's clothes in bags and set them outside. I changed the locks on the doors and confided in Carol on the phone about the recent turn of events.

She was warm and loving and spoke with a charming native Virginia drawl. "You'll shudda done this long ago, girl. That man no good fer you. Many times I seen the bruises on yer tired face and had to bite my tongue. I figgered you get tired of it all and kick him out sooner or later."

God, I loved her.

The children were more lighthearted than I had ever known them to be. "Now he can't hit you anymore." Phillip proudly held my hand as Regina did a dance with Raggedy Ann.

And when their father came by for his belongings later that day, they both ran into the kitchen and hid under the sink.

Joseph

A few months after Joseph received the letter from Michael, another one came. This one was from Rachel.

"Dearest Father," it read. "I need your help." It went on to inform him of Alan's leave—taking at Rachel's command. "I need money to feed my children. Please help me just until I graduate. Then I will be able to support them on my own. This is so difficult, but I know you won't let me down. Love forever, Rachel."

The next day Joseph wired $5,000 to his eldest daughter and never said a word to anyone.

It was extremely stuffy in the conference room. Mrs. Brown, the clinical instructor at the hospital, had called us off the floor an hour early so we could discuss the exam we would be given at school on Friday. "A review conference" she called it.

Everyone loved Mrs. Brown. She was everything any teacher could ever wish to be. She was professional, sophisticated, brilliant, compassionate, understanding, and above all else, possessed the power to motivate.

This afternoon, however, the whole class was hot with boredom, through no fault of Mrs. Brown. The disinterest the class displayed could possibly be blamed on the fact that they had all been out partying the night before, and according to my source had "hit" at least a dozen of the Lansing night clubs. "You should have come with us," they had solemnly advised me. "You need to come out of your shell of misery."

They were, of course, referring to the trauma with Alan that had led to our recent, inevitable separation. And what splendid friends they were, rallying about me with words of encouragement and notes from classes I had missed.

The soft hush of the ceiling fan, the muted sounds of distant traffic, and the rustle of papers and textbooks filtered through my befuddled mind. Ruffling through the sparse notes for Friday's exam, I saw Michael's face on every crumpled, severely scribbled page.

His aura surrounded me. Last night had been incredible. My every brain cell was saturated with thoughts of him.

By yesterday afternoon, I could wait no longer. I had phoned him at his office after class.

"Alan hit me for the last time last weekend, Michael. I made him leave and got a restraining order." A long, explosive breath kissed softly over the line.

"He has been hitting you, hasn't he?" Outraged tones. "I just knew it. You always seemed afraid of him. Dear Jesus, I'll kill him."

"Mike, it won't happen anymore. He's gone away. I won't ever let him come back."

His voice was light with emotion, "Oh, baby." Sigh. "There is a God."

Within an hour he was at the door of my dorm room. "I left work early," he spoke quietly as he brushed trembling fingers through my hair.

"I should be studying." I tried to smile, but my face felt stiff. The tempestuous emotions I felt at seeing him again made me want to weep. His touch made me weak, and I'm sure my knees quaked visibly.

"Come in," I finally spoke through stiff lips and stood aside so he could enter. *Why did I feel so awkward?*

He closed the door and reverently kissed my lips. Gently, he ran caressing fingers up my arms, over my throat and cheeks. "I've never kissed a nurse before." He chuckled softly, and I envied his remarkable composure.

For want of something to do I busied myself with tidying the already tidy dorm room, straightening the already organized desk, and closing the window and then opening it again.

"Rachel, please relax."

Michael's hushed, well-modulated voice regulated the

palpating rush of blood through my heart a bit, and my knees were no longer knocking together.

I sat down on the bed beside him, and for what seemed like an eternity we simply looked at each other. With unmistakable, almost violent conviction, his compelling gentian eyes spoke love.

"Don't look at me like that," I protested weakly as I ran gentle fingers over his Oscar DeLarenti tie.

He sighed and turned to stare unseeingly at the window. The muscle that quivered in his jaw belied the composure I had admired in him just a few moments ago.

The soft glow of twilight somehow managed to filter through the thick cloud of leaves of maple trees and ivy that flourished everywhere on the campus.

We sat in silence on the bed and watched the eerie pinkish-green shadows that danced erratically over the once beautiful, now faded and worn Oriental rug.

"How've you been?" I finally asked.

Michael tilted his head in a provocative, yet whimsical manner for a moment and looked intently into my eyes and then dropped his head in his hands and laughed quietly, bitterly.

"You have been systematically smashing my heart to tiny pieces for the last seven years and you ask me how I've been?" He answered my question with another question, speaking slowly and distinctly.

After a few moments, he lifted his head and took both my hands in his. The urgency in his grasp coursed through my fingers and up my arms like a powerful bolt of energy.

"Rachel, I have thought this over long and hard, and

I have come to an undisputable conclusion that my life is colorless without you."

Silence.

"What do you want me to do?" I finally asked.

"That is fairly obvious." He spoke in firm, yet gentle tones. "Let's go somewhere and talk about it."

Subsequently, we found ourselves seated in the corner of a quiet, out-of-the-way cafe in an antiquated part of town.

I was only faintly aware of our surroundings. The candle burned fitfully in the hand-painted glass in the center of the tiny table. There were crumbs on the tablecloth leftover from the last customer.

Michael leaned across and grasped my hands in his.

His eyes were simultaneously sad, amused, and urgent. Slowly, he looked around, inspecting the odd decorations on the walls; fishnets, shells, driftwood, and stuff like that.

"I like places like this," he said, "reminds me of my hipster days."

He ordered scotch and soda for both of us. I had to show my ID to the waitress.

"So what are we going to do?" I asked quietly, desperately.

Michael softly spoke, outrage barely suppressed in his tones.

"What are we going to do?" He laughed bitterly. "I love you. I want to live with you always. I want to have children that have your eyes and your hair. I want to grow old with you. What is holding you back? God. You're almost a free woman now. Why don't you bring your children and live with me in my condo in South Bend? Or better yet, why don't you marry me?" He threw up his hands in frustration. "Do you have any other suggestions?"

Not daring to look at him, I stared at the ice cubes in the scotch. I wanted to be with him, too. I had prayed to be with him. Yet, how could I explain the confusion in my heart?

"I can't explain how I'm feeling, Michael." I shook my head helplessly. "My heart tells me to just be with you, but I am so afraid." I hesitated for a moment and then shrugged helplessly. "Maybe it's too soon…or something."

I gazed at his downcast head. "Oh, Michael, don't you understand? I'm just trying to be fair to you."

"So, then, why don't you just be unfair to me and see how much I like it." His humor failed to disguise the pain in his voice.

For hours we sat in the cafe and talked and gazed at each other and watched the candle burn down and the ice cubes melt in the scotch.

"I have to get back to the dorm," I finally said, unwilling—even as I spoke—to end the magic of being with Michael.

He nodded and gently took my arm and guided me to his sports car parked on the cobblestone street outside the ancient cafe. Even the streetlights looked as if they came straight out of Dickens' "A Christmas Carol."

Back at the campus, Michael reached over and cradled me in his arms and kissed me fervently.

"Please come in for awhile," I said urgently, breathlessly.

Surprise and joy came slowly over his face. "Are you sure?"

"Yes! Please."

After entering my dorm room, Michael embraced me

again and murmured with the deepest conviction and fervor, his lips brushing my hair, "I will love you and comfort you."

My face was wet with tears of love and joy. Michael kissed them away and we made effortless, eloquent love. For the first time in my life I knew why it was called making love.

Michael left early the next morning. He looked at me long and hard, his eyes drinking in every detail of my face. He stroked a thumb gently across my cheekbone.

"You're beautiful," he whispered. "I love you. I'm not saying good-bye. I refuse to. When you feel like your 'head' is right, call me. Until then, I'll wait."

By the grace of God and the convenience of an excellent short-term memory, I passed the final exam in psychology that Friday.

A month later, classes ended for the summer. "Now we can have our mommy back," Phillip informed Regina happily.

chapter 27

That summer passed by all too swiftly. On hot, sunny days the children and I went swimming in many of the local beaches. Our bodies became beautifully tanned, the children's hair became streaked with gold, and mine turned amber. The regular bouts of swimming left my body toned and slim. For the first time in my life, I recognized the beauty of my physical self without feelings of guilt.

That summer was a time of stabilizing. Congruent with the somnolence of the eddying heat was the recognition that I could be strong alone. I no longer needed the crutch of Alan's presence.

That summer was a time of reflection. The dust, the

soothing, penetrating heat, and the very smells of summer reflected the idyllic summers of my childhood. As the children splashed joyously in the shallow water close to the shore, I reminisced about the secret bathing expeditions in the river in Berne.

I reflected on where I was then, and where I was now, and found that I had changed little in my heart. Perhaps not at all. The beauty was that now I could express my beliefs in thought and action with out being scorned or scolded.

I thought of my parents, of my father especially, and how he continued in quiet desperation, to live his life to gain the respect of his parents and the family. Perhaps he had long ago accepted a life of repression and now even gained satisfaction and happiness from it. Once, long ago, during a chess game in the moonlight, he told me so. I hadn't believed him then, but now I wondered. Perhaps he now viewed it as a stimulating challenge and thought of it as a way of proving his self-worth. I thought of Michael and of that last magical evening together and felt no guilt. Only joy.

That summer was a time of prayer and contemplation. Not a day passed that I wouldn't pray for my parents' acceptance of me. I prayed for God to bless Michael in his work, his life. I prayed that I could be with him.

In the evenings, with the children, soft and loveable in their nightclothes, I would pray for their safety and salvation, for peace in their hearts, in mine and Michael's hearts, and in my parents' hearts.

"What does that mean, Mamma?" Phillip would ask often. "Why do you pray for peace in Mum und Dat Streikers' hearts? And who is Michael?"

Oh, it is so important. How does one explain this to a child, I would think. *If they have peace, perhaps they will accept me for who I am.* Then I would refrain from answering his latter question.

With an arm clasped around each of their dear little bodies, I would lie quiet for hours, listening to their soft breathing rhythmically breaking the stillness of the night.

Late in August, a few days before classes resumed at school, Hannah called again.

She was distraught. "Rachel," she sobbed. "I'm being pressured into joining the church, and I don't know what to do. Please help me."

White-hot anger left me lightheaded for a moment.

"Of course, I'll help you, Hannah," I answered fervently. She was two hundred miles away. How would I help her? "Tell me slowly, what is happening," I urged Hannah to give a more coherent account.

Hannah had grown into a beautiful woman, albeit shy, unassuming, and troubled.

She had few friends, although she wasn't in the slightest bit interested in Margorie's daring to add just a bit of forbidden ruffle to the sleeves of her dress, or in Naomi's pink nail color (taboo!), or in Bertha's wrist watch (worldly!), she nonetheless tried to fit into the world of her peers. She secretly viewed them all as simple, immature, and easily manipulated. They all secretly labeled her a snob.

There came that time every spring when young people would attend instruction classes where they would study Amish doctrine preparing for later baptism into the church.

When her peers reached the enlightened age of sixteen,

they were expected to "follow" instruction class, and did just that. Hannah hesitated to do so. Is this what she really wanted—this Amish way? Her time of questioning struck a now familiar chord of fear in her parents' hearts. (What? Not again!) So now, with renewed zeal, they applied pressure to already-anxious, adolescent Hannah to be baptized into the Amish faith.

And when these efforts appeared to be failing, Joseph called in the troops. Before long, the church elders were stopping by the Streiker home at generously scheduled intervals, administering large doses of well-meant admonition upon the young, defenseless Hannah.

"Rachel," Hannah sobbed now over the wires, "I felt so out-numbered. I finally gave in." She drew a shuddering breath. "What on earth can I do?"

"Hannah, you are so young, you have ample time to think about what you want to do with your life. If you decide to leave two or three years from now, then you can do so then." I doubted that my dreadfully inadequate response would be much reassurance to the girl on the other end of the line. My own sense of helplessness angered me even further.

"I love you, Rachel."

"I love you too, *mein liebshken.* Everything will work out in due time."

"I hope so."

A few weeks later I received a letter from Mother. With relief apparent between every line, she wrote that Hannah was now going to instruction class, preparing for baptism into the culture. She obviously wasn't aware of the recent phone conversation between Hannah and I.

She wrote how Hannah's attitude had become more peaceful and content. Bitterly, I guessed Hannah's attitude to be more accurately described as quietly despondent and indifferent. In addition she expressed, *"Of course, we are shocked and deeply shamed about you and Alan. Those poor children, what they must be going through. You must know how wrong it is—what you are doing. I hope God has mercy on your soul. Love, Mother."*

The rain beat, insistent and fretful, on the windshield. Eagerly I pressed onward, peering through the flooded glass the wipers could not keep dry. I was anxious to pick up the children at Aunt Carol's house. This was the fall of 1981. I was in the second half of nurses training.

We were fast approaching midterms; and most of the student population was in a frenzy, trying to cram in last minute studying. I'd had a sick knot at the pit of my stomach for the last week, the kind of knot I always got around exam time. I had mentioned as much to Jean in the microbiology lab earlier that day.

"You always say you're worried about exams and end up with higher scores than most of us. I think you play this act for attention," she snarled at me, running red fingernails through her ash blond permanent.

At the present time, Jean was caught up in a quite mad infatuation with one of the college professors and was feeling thwarted in love because he didn't return her attentions.

I pushed those thoughts from my mind as I entered Carol's driveway. I was glad it was Friday and I had the weekend with the children. Carol greeted me at the door, her round face glowing with welcome. I quickly embraced her plump frame and then bent to receive joyous kisses and hugs from Phillip and Regina. They were both trying to talk at once, excitedly informing me about their activities in school.

Phillip was now in first grade; Regina was in nursery school. They followed me into the kitchen, still talking about their various experiences at school. Carol stood by the sink, cutting up vegetables for a stew. The kitchen was warm and misty from cooking and smelled of onions like Grandmother Streiker's used to.

I sank wearily into one of her vinyl kitchen chairs and watched her fat, nimble fingers pare potatoes and carrots. When the pot of vegetables was prepared, she set it on the stove to simmer. With that, she instructed Phillip and Regina to pick up the school papers they had strewn over the living room floor. Then she turned to me, hands on hips, an expression of amusement, pity, and outrage tightening up her generous mouth.

"You're gonna kill yourself, girl. You know that? You is workin' too hard." She paced back and forth in the kitchen, pretending to be busy putting dishes away, her short, obese frame moving with surprising agility. "Oh, I've seen your kind before, all work and no play. Why don't you get you some sort of a social life? Maybe with this Mike fella the kids told me about?"

I smiled wearily at this precious friend, self-appointed mother.

"We did go to the zoo a few weeks back," I said meekly. "Mike took the children and me."

"Humph," she snorted in the most unladylike fashion. "You gotta get you some romance. I'll take the children for a weekend, and you go somewhere with that young man. When do I gets to meet him?"

"Soon."

"You know what your problem is, Rachel? Girl, you is afraid. You gotta let go of the past and learn to trust and love. It ain't natural for a girl like you to be alone."

Presently she put a plate of cornbread (spread with butter) on the table in front of me. "Eat," she commanded. "You is plumb skinny." (Shades of Mother.)

Michael. *Love.* Our relationship had been platonic ever since the night in the dorm. We did nice things together with the children. Outings at the park; pizza; the zoo.

The children eagerly awaited Mike's every visit and would greet him with wild abandon. ("What are we going to do today, Mike?") And he would give into their every whim.

I would laugh accusingly at Mike and say, "Is this how you plan on winning my affection?"

We spent Sunday afternoons at Emmanuel's house. Emmanuel loved Michael. They played music together, but Emmanuel's Amish bride didn't approve.

Emmanuel, who was now married and had a lovely daughter and lived on a farm close to Nappanee, soon became my sternest, most loving critic. We went to visit him and his family often; and every time he would fondly, but firmly, lecture me about the rapid drifting away and backsliding that I was doing. Somehow, I never resented his lectures. He meant well. Mike would shrug helplessly and smile. Emmanuel's dark handsome face was fast becoming thin and worn from the hard work of buying a farm and then the struggle to make enough money off the land to make the payments. But he was brave and never gave up. Sometimes I glimpsed a deep discontent in him, reminding me acutely and painfully of my father.

He had given me the beautifully crafted guitar he had made when he got married. It was not kosher for a married Amish man to own a guitar. So when we went down to visit Emmanuel, I would usually sneak it along and he, Mike, and I would sing and make music together just like old times; right after his lectures to me about my aggressive, liberal behavior of late.

Presently, with my thoughts of Emmanuel ended and with my stomach full of cornbread, the children still chattering, we bid Carol "See you Monday" and went home to the house in the woods.

chapter 28

That year the children and I spent Christmas alone. It was the first time we didn't go home to my parents for the holiday. I felt a terrible sadness, as with anguish I realized that an era of my life had come to an end. The beautiful traditions of my family were now a thing of the past. Now my children and I would have to build our own.

The day before Christmas, I received a small package in the mail. Even before I opened it, I knew who it was from. Inside was a lovely silver locket. With trembling fingers, I opened the locket. The strength drained from me as I gazed at Michael's poignant face. I hadn't heard from him in months.

He had finally informed me toward the last days of summer that he was tired of being kept on hold.

A tiny note was enclosed with the locket. It simply read, "You are always on my mind."

With tears streaming down my face, I dialed Michael's office number.

"Michael isn't in," the impersonal voice on the other end of the line said. "He is spending Christmas with some friends in California. He said something about wanting to get as far away from home as possible."

Silently, I placed the receiver back on its cradle.

"Oh, Michael," I wept softly. "I love you."

That year we had our first Christmas tree. The children and I cut it down from the forest behind our house. The needles on its branches were terribly sharp, and it was dreadfully lopsided; but it was the most wonderful tree ever!

We decorated the tree with cranberries, popcorn, tinsel, and even a string of electric lights. Mike's crystal nestled in splendor on the top branch. How wonderful it all was! I bought the children the best presents ever, and we ate ham and dressing and pumpkin pie.

Watching the children open their gifts on Christmas morning and later as we read from the Bible about the birth of Christ, I realized that we could find peace, right there in our lovely country home in the woods.

With or without the acceptance and respect of my parents, I could be content. I remembered Mike quoting Shakespeare to me a thousand light years ago "...to thine own self be true." Now I understood. How utterly good it felt.

After the gifts were opened and the children had

thoroughly investigated their treasures, Regina came up beside me and embraced me warmly. "Oh, Mamma, this is the bestest Christmas ever!"

"Oh, yes," Phillip added absentmindedly as he raced miniature sports cars around the new electric race track.

The spirit of good will was with us. It was in the ham, sweet breads, and other trimmings I had lovingly prepared. It rang in the albums of classic Christmas hymns we played on the stereo.

It radiated from the sparkling, asymmetrical tree in the corner of the living room. And most of all, there was acceptance, tolerance, and freedom—the beginnings of a heritage for my children.

We went sledding in the afternoon at Bonneyville Mill Park and then tried our luck at ice-skating on a local pond. By six-thirty in the evening, the children fell asleep on the living room floor. Regina had "Baby-That-A-Way" clasped in her arms; Phillip still had the control handle for the electric racetrack in his hands.

After the children were in bed, I walked for miles in the forest. A million thoughts filled my mind. "Merry Christmas, Michael," I spoke softly to the pines. I contemplated our first Christmas alone. All the pain and anguish of remembering and missing the Christmases and traditions past tore my heart in tiny pieces. Never had I felt sadness so awful, so intense. It was hot and all consuming.

I remembered the Christmas story my family had read from the German Bible. I remembered the feasts, the endless singing and merrymaking at my grandparents' house back in

Berne. I remembered and longed for the Christmas that was and wept convulsively.

It was only because of the peace I had found that I was able to cry. The walls were gone—the brick walls covered with ivy.

I walked back to the house, got into bed, and slept a deep and dreamless sleep.

Excitement was high on the college campus. Graduation was finally upon us. I could scarcely breathe.

The conversation in the cafeteria, on the campus concrete walkways, and in the classrooms before exams was wild and incoherent. High emotions raced through every corridor. Some students walked into the halls where the finals were held with disgusting confidence, others were pale and shaking with anxiety.

I felt something close to stunned shock. I had really made it. I remembered Father's words, "If you want to do something badly enough, you will do it."

My heart filled with gratitude to my father for instilling a confidence in me that never died. I remembered his defense of me so many years ago at the barn-raising in Berne. "No one will every break her spirit."

I remembered his standing up for me against Alan's father when Aaron had degraded and defamed me for running to Mike's parents. "Oh, Father, aren't you proud of me?" I whispered countless times, convinced that he could hear me in his heart.

Graduation Day seemed to last forever, moments

suspended in time. I felt out of touch with the event, as though this couldn't really be happening to me. I felt no soaring ecstasy, only relief, gratitude, and deep contentment.

The words of the ceremony speaker echoed through my mind, *the end of so much and the beginning of so much more.* All speakers must say those words graduation. That's what someone had said when I received my high school diploma.

Proudly, I smiled at my two beautiful children sitting with Aunt Carol only a few yards away. With them were some close friends, and Marion.

I can scarcely remember going through the mechanics of receiving my diploma, having the nursing pin fastened to my white gown, or the dean's words to me. "You've come a long way, Rachel." She smiled in triumph as though my success were partly her victory.

In a daze, I touched the gold pin and lovingly clasped the diploma. It felt so good! Hot tears of thankfulness and joy flowed down my cheeks. If only my parents could see me now. I had sent gilded invitations to them and had not received a reply, not even a congratulatory comment.

Later, as we had cake and punch at Carol's, she embraced me reverently. "I am so proud of you, girl."

My face was drenched in tears. "I'm thinking about my parents and how much I wish they could have been here tonight."

Carol nodded understandingly. "They were here honey. You can be sure of that."

Joseph

Joseph Streiker carefully inspected the gilded invitation as he turned it over and over in his hands. Sarah admired the script, touching the gold letters reverently.

"It gives us great pleasure to extend this invitation to you, concerning your daughter's graduation ceremony, to be held…to be graduating with high honors…" It was inscribed on parchment in great flourishes.

"Oh, I do so wish we could go." Sarah sighed wistfully and then flushed guiltily at Joseph's reprimanding glance.

He, too, longed to attend Rachel's graduation, but he could never say that. Joseph Streiker would stand firm. Any affirmation or recognition of Rachel's achievement could result in his losing another child to the "world." First Rachel, and then, just this spring, Hannah.

Beautiful Hannah. Only eighteen. She had met and married an "outsider" boy and went with him to Tucson where he was attending medical school. Martin Boyle was a nice boy, came from a good farm family. But he wasn't an Amish boy. Joseph's parents were distraught. What on earth was happening to their eldest son's children? They concluded that "we must certainly be in the Last Days—so many people falling away from God."

Joseph thought of Hannah's resistance at being baptized into the Amish faith. Perhaps it was his fault that she "ran away" to Arizona. He shuddered.

Sarah gazed at him. "Maybe we shouldn't have pushed the girls so much," she observed quietly.

Joseph was silent. He thought of the note Rachel had inserted in the invitation—addressed to him only. "Dearest Father," it read, "How can I ever thank you? If not for you, I would not be holding this diploma. Love and see you soon, Rachel."

He would never tell Sarah about the note. He smiled wistfully at his wife and kissed her.

Then Joseph went out to the cornfield behind the immense cattle barn and wept.

chapter 29

A year had passed since graduation. I had found employment at a local hospital, and once again Aunt Carol was babysitting my children. An occasional letter from Iris informed me of Michael's progress. He had moved from South Bend and was now living in California and "investing in real estate or vineyards or some such thing."

Mine and Alan's divorce had been finalized six months. It had come about by mutual consent. He had found a girlfriend and was now living with her in an apartment in Elkhart. Occasionally, he would come by for the children, and they would reluctantly spend the day with him at the zoo, the mall or Bonneyville Mill Park. The children and

I remained in the house in the woods and spent our time befriending wild rabbits and swimming in the river at a local park right by the sign that read, "No Swimming."

That fall, upon Alan's insistence, the home in the country was sold. He said he wanted to help his girlfriend buy a house. The children's initial disappointment and sadness at once again having to leave their home turned to excitement when I, alongside a local realtor, showed them a darling, three-bedroom bungalow in a quiet suburb of Elkhart that I anticipated buying with my proceeds of the sale.

"This is a nice place," Phillip announced in a quiet business-like manner after carefully inspecting every inch of the home. Goodness, he was the man of the house. He had reached the ripe age of nine!

"Mama, look! It has a window you can sit in!" Regina's lilting voice penetrated my amused contemplations of Phillip.

"That's a bay window, honey. Isn't it wonderful?"

Within a few weeks, the transaction was complete. With the assistance of Carol, Marion, Aunt Leah, and a few strong-shouldered orderlies I had befriended at the hospital, the move was made.

The children and I happily decorated the lovely blue house with white shutters.

Then we painted the door red. "In the spring we'll plant petunias and geraniums and irises all around the house," I informed my two helpers.

They nodded in unison. Phillip suggested a bird feeder, and Regina thought a birdbath would be nice.

And in the spring, we did just that. We went to K-mart

and purchased paint, brushes, birdseed, and a bird feeder shaped like the Eiffel Tower.

Then in the center of the tiny front yard we placed a mock Grecian marble birdbath and planted pink and white geraniums around it.

Everything was wonderful.

"Liar." This was the response of Doris when I told her of the utopia my life had become. Doris was a nurse I worked with on the Coronary Care Unit. "There is something or someone missing in your life, Rachel. I see it in your eyes when you get that faraway look whenever you're supposed to be charting or evaluating telemetry stripes or…you know… anytime you have time to sit down and think."

Shrugging with pseudo-nonchalance, I failed to meet her knowing gaze. "Maybe."

"Maybe, bullshit!" She bobbed her blond curls. Nurses do have such foul mouths, I observed silently.

I smiled lovingly at her, and presently we exited cafeteria left and headed back upstairs to the "dawn madhouse." I sure did love her.

"You swear like a sailor, Doris."

She pressed six on the elevator panel and smiled engagingly as the doors swished shut.

"I know. Isn't it damn awful?"

That afternoon I came home to find a letter from Hannah. She and her husband were now both starving med students in some university in Arizona, yet blissfully happy and desperately in love.

Dear Rachel,

   I think of you often. Martin and I are both either working or studying. Last weekend we took some time off and motored up to Northern California and toured through a winery. It was very interesting. They make those wine coolers there. We got free samples!

   Amazingly enough, the owner is a native of Indiana. We didn't get to meet him but his name is Michael Byron or something like that.

   Wouldn't that be something if we would by chance know him? I wish we did. He could help Martin and me through med school and maybe we could eat something other than canned beans and hot dogs! There was this huge white house with pillars right on the vineyard grounds up on a hill. But it had an iron fence and locked gates, so we couldn't get very close. The guide told us the owner, Byron, lives there.

   Anyway, Martin said we could maybe go mountain climbing again soon. He thinks we have to do things like that to relieve stress.

   Mom and Dad write more often now. The tone of their letters is almost congenial. They want us to come home to visit this summer.

Love,
Hannah

I scarcely saw the words in the latter part of the letter. Michael. Michael in the cafe long ago…"buy some vineyard in California…drown myself in the cup like Mozart did."

For what seemed like hours I stared blindly at the words in Hannah's letter. After a time, I went into the tiny kitchen and made a cup of tea. The children would be home from school soon and Amo the Amish dog was whining to be fed. There was dinner to be prepared and my legs were so weary from running around CCU all day I wanted to weep.

Mike was living in some palace in northern California, making wine coolers and probably married to some stepford wife who played tennis and painted her nails mauve.

———————

"Mrs. Bower, your husband will be fine." I was attempting, and failing miserably, to placate the distraught wife of a critical congestive heart failure that had arrived a few hours before. He had been stabilized with IV Lasix and Lanoxin, but my nerves were screaming.

At that moment Doris appeared at the doorway, "We need you at the desk, Rachel."

I gave Mrs. Bower a reassuring hug. "Would you please excuse me for a moment?" She nodded and continued sobbing into an already-drenched Kleenex.

Doris had "I told you so" written all over her face.

"What's the problem?" I hurried up the hall beside her, brushing straggling hairs off my face. *God, I must look awful,* I thought.

"There is a man here to see you. We told him CCU was off limits to everyone but family, but he insisted." Doris rolled her eyes heavenward. "God, he is a doll. I swear those are imported Italian sports clothes." She gazed pointedly at the man standing at the desk.

I followed her look and stopped dead in my tracks.

Michael! And I am looking like a freight train.

At that moment he turned and our eyes locked. I was rooted to the spot where I had stopped, and suddenly all the busy sounds of the unit became muted and distant. The hums of telemetry became the lyrical music of Mike's guitar in Grandma Shelhorn's garden, and the fluorescent lighting turned into the candlelight of the cafe where Mike told me of vineyards and Mozart.

"Rachel. I've come back for you." Michael was embracing me, touching my face then embracing me again.

"How did you find me?" I asked, numb with relief and ecstasy.

"Mother kept me well informed." He smiled his forever-whimsical smile.

I became aware of Doris off to the side, drinking in every detail of Mike's charismatic person.

"I always knew there was someone," she observed smugly.

I giggled like a schoolgirl. "Wait until the children find out." I looked beseeching at Mike and then at the clock. One hour left for my shift.

"I'll wait," he said. "I've been waiting for ten years. What's an hour more?"

epilogue

Last week I went back to Berne. I met my parents at my Grandparents Streikers.' It's been a long time.

The volcanic emotions that were so overpowering during the years of transition have all dissipated—as have the days of my magical childhood.

Father and I walked under the apple trees and smelled the lilacs as I wept bittersweet tears of nostalgia. He clasped my hand in silent regret, a sad longing in his eyes for time wasted and what could have been.

"Hannah loves living in Phoenix," he said. "She and Martin are so happily married." Silence. "We never see her."

Hannah, as I, is a disappointment to my father.

Emmanuel, on the other hand, has become devout in his service to the Amish community and frequently visits my parents. He is the apple of Father's eye.

The milking barn is just as I had remembered it—with its cool, whitewashed concrete brushing under my bare feet and rancid aroma of silage. Slowly, we walked back to the wooden-floored porch with its ancient porch swing, much like the one where the moonlight chess games were held so long ago.

My throat was tight, and I couldn't speak an answer to Father's simple statement, "I'm glad you came to Berne."

Grandmother has changed. She's become older, of course, but she has changed in a different way. I suppose I'm very sensitive because I know how she once admired me. Grandfather, too, doesn't feel as close to me as once. "Tootsie," he used to call me. Such a rugged, forbidding man, small wonder that my father could be awed by Grandfather's imposing presence. For all his intimidating qualities, he was a kind man, made all the more endearing by his limp, the result of childhood polio.

My family sees me as a "worldly" person.

"Rachel is at the university now, we hear. My, what will become of her? And what's worse, she has a boyfriend in California whom she flies out to be with every time she turns around. A wealthy wine-maker or something like that. Tsk, Tsk."

We enter the quiet serenity of the kitchen where Grandmother is doing the lunch dishes, with the assistance of my mother and Marietta, who married an Amish boy and lives near my parents and has babies on a yearly basis.

"Does the old homestead seem the same?" Grandmother

queries and then looks quickly away when she notices my anguish-filled eyes.

Ach, Grosmutter, ich hab nicht gevist es ich so zeit, lang hab. I sob convulsively. ("I didn't know how homesick I was.")

———

It has been almost twelve years now. I sit and drink the tea she has prepared, spearmint and honey. No one sits with me; still they carry on the shunning practice.

Nonetheless, I no longer have the feeling I am a leper. I am treated with respect, however tempered it is with condescension.

And so there we are, in Grandmother's kitchen, with its gleaming copper pans, blue-clothed oak table, and enormous iron cooking range. Just like times past? No, of course not.

I have lived centuries since those lazy summer days of long ago. That was when I wasn't jaded by the morals and concepts of the "outside." When I loved and trusted the whole world. When I had never heard of the universal controversies of abortion and gay rights.

Oh, God, have I sacrificed too much? My heart is heavy.

No. I haven't. Because now I see only the beauty in the simplicity of "their" life, instead of being embittered by its rigidity and suppression.

As I rise to leave, Father embraces me. He has never done that before.

"So, when shall we all come to Berne again?" he asks.

"Oh, Father," I cry with utter, complete relief. "Very soon, don't you think?"

And I'm sure we will.